Unexpected Love

The Silver Fox Falls Series

By

Rose Bak

Table of Contents

Amy 1

Sam 7

Amy 11

Sam 15

Amy 19

Sam 24

Amy 29

Sam 34

Amy 39

Sam 43

Amy 47

Sam 52

Amy 58

Sam 64

Amy 69

Sam 74

Epilogue – Amy 78

Special Preview 81

Other Books by Rose Bak 84

About the Author 87

Copyright

---

1. https://paperorpixels.com/

About This Book

She's avoided commitment for fifty-six years. There's no way she's going to let some guy she just met put a ring on her finger now!

Amy

After my landlord sells our apartment building, leaving me homeless, my best friend Julie convinces me to rent her condo at the Silver Falls Active Living Community. I wouldn't have even considered moving into a fifty-five and older community, but I'm getting a great deal on the rent. And then there's all the hot older guys living there. I guess there's a reason the residents call this place "Silver Fox Falls".

Things are changing with my best friend getting married and my big move. I'm determined to make a fresh start and be open to new friendships. Except with the guy next door, that is. He's a shameless flirt who has a different woman in his place every day of the week. He's noisy and bossy and somehow I keep running into him during all my most embarrassing moments. So why am I so obsessed with him?

Sam

I fell in love with Amy the instant I set eyes on her. Unfortunately, the curvy beauty hates me. Her stubborn independence and ability to trip over her own feet make me want to take care of her, but it's the heat in her eyes that tells me she's feeling the same attraction that I am.

Valentine's Day is coming and there's only one woman I want to be my date for the big event. But Amy is determined to keep me at arm's length. I guess it's time to pull out my best charm offensive, because I'm not going to rest until she's mine – forever.

Welcome to Silver Fox Falls, where residents soon learn that midlife is the best time to find true love. Expect spunky and independent women, charming and sexy older men, and nosy neighbors who are intent on matchmaking to help get their friends to a sweet happily ever after.

Join My Mailing List

Join Rose Bak's mailing list at bit.ly/RoseBakNewsletter[2]. You'll get a free book and be the first to hear about all the latest releases, special sales, free books, and funny stories about my dog.

Dedication

To all the people who, like me, manage to trip over their own feet on a regular basis. You're still cool, clumsy girl.

Amy

"Harder Sam, harder!"

My, well, I wasn't sure what to call him...boyfriend? hook-up? friend with benefits? sped up his thrusts, his hips slamming against mine hard enough that I was sliding up the cushions of the couch.

Damn, he was so good at this. I was close, so close. I used my heels at his waist to pull him in tighter, the movement arching my hips into a slightly different angle. Oh yes, that was it. Our skin slapped against each other, making an obscene sound. It only turned me on more.

Sam arched his back, veins sticking out in his neck in a way that I knew meant he was holding himself back, waiting for me to come first. Sometimes he was a nice guy. Of course other times, he was a bossy asshole.

My back arched and my body shuddered beneath him as my orgasm hit me. "Sam!"

Warmth infused all my cells, followed closely by what could only be called euphoria. Even though we'd only been dating for a few weeks, we were amazingly in sync, as if we'd been exploring each other's bodies for years.

"I'm coming," Sam grunted, his pace slowing as he pushed deeper inside me and released his cum in long spurts.

"Amy!"

Suddenly he stiffened above me, his face twisting in pain. "Ah!"

Sam collapsed on top of me, dead weight, then rolled off, falling onto the floor next to the couch. He was breathing heavily, his skin ashen, his expression pure agony.

Holy crap, was he having a heart attack? Did I kill him by having sex with him?

"Sam, what is it? Is it your heart?"

He closed his eyes as he curled onto his side. "No, but I think you broke me."

"Oh my God! We broke your penis?"

I'd seen this on an episode of Grey's Anatomy once, but I didn't think that really happened in real life.

"No, my back."

***

Seven weeks earlier...

"Are you sure you're okay with me renting out your condo?" I asked Julie for about the tenth time.

My best friend grunts at me over the box she's carrying.

"I told you before, Amy, you're doing me a huge favor. With me staying at Dante's penthouse, you renting my condo will help me a lot. I've got a mortgage to pay you know. Plus, I won't have to worry about some rando destroying my investment."

"Why did you say you're staying at Dante's?" I asked, picking up on her odd choice of words. "I thought you guys were going to live there after the wedding?"

My uber practical best friend had shocked the hell out of me by falling in love with Dante, a guy she met right after she moved here to the Silver Falls Active Living Community. She'd hated the guy at first after she overheard him acting like an idiot, but once they moved past that they'd both fallen fast. She'd lived here less than three months.

A few days ago, on Christmas he proposed to her and she said yes, to everyone's surprise. Including Dante's I suspect. She probably should have made him work a little harder for it, but that wasn't in my best friend's nature. After a shitty marriage that left her raising two kids on her own, I was glad that Julie had finally found a guy who treated her well and was so obviously head over heels in love with her that it made my heart pinch every time I was around them.

"Oh yes, but it still feels like I'm a guest at his place, you know?" Julie explained. "But we agreed to do some redecorating at Dante's house so it will feel like my place too. A little color in the place will help immensely. The guy likes his blacks and greys."

"Well you did a great job decorating this place," I said, looking around at the warm and comfortable condo.

My friend's redecorating skills were on point. She'd made what could have been a boring beige box into a vibrant sanctuary. It was much nicer than the place I'd been living in forever. There wasn't one thing in here that came from a thrift shop. Everything was tasteful and classy.

Even after my best friend moved here, I would have never guessed I'd end up at Silver Falls—or Silver Fox Falls as the residents called it, due to the high numbers of hot older bachelors living here – but right before Christmas my landlord had dropped the bomb on me. He'd sold the duplex I was living in, and my neighbors and I had sixty days to find a new place to live.

I knew the landlord was getting older and preparing to retire, but it had never occurred to me that he'd actually sell the place.

When I'd moved into the duplex twenty years ago it had been fully furnished, so I was also losing most of my furniture. It was shitty old furniture, but I'd had it for so long I'd forgotten that, like the apartment, it wasn't mine.

It was a gut punch, especially after so many years living there, but then again, I'd allowed inertia to keep me in that place years after I could have afforded something nicer. If I'd been smart, I would have bought a nice little house or condo years ago before real estate prices skyrocketed.

I liked Silver Falls just fine though. It was a planned community specifically for people aged fifty-five and older, offering an active lifestyle as well as a supportive community to age in place. Julie was always talking about the mixers and Zumba classes and walking groups.

It wasn't cheap to live there, but everything was immaculately maintained, and the owners took good care of all the residents. Julie had given me a good deal on the rent, only asking that I cover her mortgage and condo fees and pay my own utilities. It was a little more money than I'd been paying at my old place, but definitely a step up, and less than I'd pay for something comparable elsewhere.

Julie put down the box she was carrying and came around to take my box, setting it on the ground. Putting an arm around my shoulders, she gave me a side hug.

"This is going to be great for us, Ames. You'll be close by again, just like when we were roommates in college. There's so much to do here you won't feel isolated. I know you've been kind of lonely the last few years."

I'd never mentioned feeling lonely, but Julie and I had been friends since freshman year of high school. Over the years we'd learned to read each other quite well.

The truth was I sometimes felt lonely, increasingly so over the last few years. I'd noticed as I'd gotten older that my circle of friends had gotten smaller and smaller. People would move away or get busy with their families and suddenly months would go by without us talking. Except for Julie, we'd remained close through thick and thin.

But the fact was I couldn't remember the last time I'd made a new friend. I didn't have a hard time finding someone to date though. I might be fifty-six, but I looked at least ten years younger. I'd fallen into the habit of filling my lonely hours with men just to distract myself, but even that had grown old.

Silver Falls was going to be a new start for me. I was bound to make friends here.

We finished bringing in the rest of my boxes. Thankfully Julie was leaving most of her furniture behind for me to use. I really needed to buy some furniture of my own, but I figured I'd use Julie's for now.

Really, it was amazing how little I had in the way of belongings even after twenty years in the same apartment. My boxes were filled mostly with household items, clothes, and shoes. Lots of shoes. Then again, I was not a person to hold onto things. I hated tchotchkes and clutter, and I was a Marie Kondo aficionado long before she became a household name in America. It wouldn't take me too long to unpack.

After extracting a promise that I would join her and Dante for dinner, Julie headed out. I was just closing the door when I noticed a piece of paper on the floor. Thinking that one of us must have dropped it, I walked into the hallway to pick it up – and promptly stepped on it instead, making my foot slide across the smooth carpet.

I windmilled my arms, trying to keep my balance, then jumped as I heard a deep voice say behind me, "Easy there."

The next thing I knew, strong hands grabbed my upper arms from behind, holding me steady and keeping me upright. I was wearing a short sleeved tee shirt and the pressure of those fingers burned through my flesh.

"Oops," I laughed, extricating myself and turning to greet my rescuer. "Thanks for catching me."

I looked up – way up – into a pair of dark brown eyes. Holy cow. I was starting to understand why people called this place Silver Fox Falls. The guy was about my age, maybe a little older, with black and silver hair, a short salt and pepper beard, and firm mouth bracketed by little grooves. He was tall and slim but with some muscle definition.

There was something about him that immediately caught my interest, and it wasn't just the fact that he had nice forearms, although I'd always been a sucker for forearms.

"Who are you?" he asked. "I haven't seen you around here before."

Something about his tone grated on my nerves but I forced a friendly smile. "Hi, I'm Amy, I just moved in."

I pointed towards my door.

The man was giving me the most unnerving stare, like I was a bug under a microscope. When he didn't respond I prompted, "And you are?"

"Oh, sorry. I'm Sam, your next door neighbor. Welcome to Silver Falls."

Just then a younger woman walked up to us wearing a tight dress and way more perfume than anyone needed.

"Hey Sam," she said in a pouty voice. "Are you ready for me?"

He gave the woman an indulgent smile.

"Hi Denise, yes, let's get to it."

I watched as Sam and the woman headed into the apartment next door to mine, feeling a stab of disappointment. Apparently Sam was one of those guys who dated women young enough to be his daughter. It figured.

Sam reached his door and turned back with a nod. "See you later, Amy. Try to watch where you're going, okay?"

Asshole.

Sam

I'd never been hit by a train before, but I'm pretty sure that particular experience would feel exactly like what I felt like now. It was like some force had smashed into me and rearranged all my cells, leaving me scrambling to create something fresh and new.

Amy.

I'd walked out of my place to meet my client just in time to see Amy slide on something on the carpet. Grabbing her arms to keep her upright had been instinct, but the tingling sensation when my fingers touched her was something else altogether. I'd felt an intense attraction before I even saw her face. Then she'd turned and I'd looked into her big blue eyes and forgotten how to speak.

She was a tiny little thing, short and super curvy. Her generous ass was encased in yoga pants that she'd paired with a tight knit tee shirt that clung to her breasts. They were a bit large for her small frame, but still perfect. She was perfect.

Her skin was creamy white, making her eyes seem even larger, and she had the cutest little button nose over her cupid's bow mouth. Her hair was shorter than I usually liked on a woman, dark brown and styled in a spiky pixie cut, but somehow it was perfect for her. I'd spent a sum total of three minutes with the woman and already knew she was a firecracker. The kind of woman who made men work hard to earn her attention.

She was also the exact woman I'd been looking for my entire life, although I didn't know it until I saw her. At sixty years old, I'd pretty much given up on finding a soul mate, but I guess fate thought I needed to wait until I was ready for love.

I'd heard through the grapevine that my neighbor Julie was renting out her condo. I'd met her a few times, but she hadn't been there long enough for us to get to know each other particularly well. Soon after she moved in, she fell for Dante, the millionaire developer who'd built Silver Falls, and no doubt his giant penthouse in another building was much more preferable than the modest one bedroom unit she'd purchased next door to me.

"Hey Sam. Are you ready for me?"

Denise saying my name brought me out of my daydreams. I'd have time to get to know Amy later, for now I needed to focus on my client.

"Hi Denise, yes, let's get to it."

I led Denise towards my front door. When I turned back to Amy and admonished her to be careful, she gave me a look that could freeze fire. My future wife clearly did not like to be told what to do. I wondered if that included the bedroom. I wasn't into BDSM or anything, but I'd been told I was a bit dominant.

Then again, I wouldn't mind if she wanted to dominate me…

Focus on your client, Sam, I admonished myself. *You have work to do.*

After I finished my session with my client, my thoughts immediately turned back to Amy. I found myself straining to hear what was going on next door. I didn't hear a thing, making me wonder if Amy had gone somewhere because while these were nice units, you could still hear at least a little bit through the walls. More than once I'd heard the telltale sounds of Julie and Dante going at it next door, including one memorable time when her adult kids had walked in on them…

Chastising myself for acting like a teenaged boy with a crush, I forced myself to stop trying to eavesdrop on Amy. Instead, I made my dinner and then read for a while before going to bed.

The next morning I was lifting weights at the Silver Falls residents' private gym when I heard someone swear. It was early still, just after six, and there usually weren't a lot of people in the gym at this hour. Curious, I looked around the corner in time to see Amy lifting her shirt up off her body, revealing a soft belly and a fuchsia sports bra. My cock twitched in my shorts at the sight.

"Are you okay?" I asked.

Amy jumped, dropping an open water bottle on the floor. Since she'd already spilled most of it on herself, there wasn't too much left. Still, the floor was wet, and I didn't want her to slip. She seemed a little bit accident prone.

"Wait here," I instructed.

Crossing to the other side of the room, I returned with a few towels, handing two to her and taking another one to mop up the water on the floor. She squatted to help, somehow knocking her forehead against mine, then falling back on her ass on the floor.

"Jesus, you're a menace," I teased, rubbing my forehead.

She gave me the stink eye.

"I didn't ask you to help," she grumbled.

"So, you're a morning person then?" I guessed.

She sighed. "I'm sorry. I decided I'd use my new apartment with its close-by gym as an opportunity to start new and healthier habits, including working out before I go into the office. Unfortunately, I was still half asleep and didn't secure the lid on my water bottle correctly."

"Understandable," I said as I mopped up the rest of the water.

"On the bright side, cold water does wonders to wake a person up," she joked.

I stood up and offered her a hand. "Let me help you up."

She hesitated long enough that I didn't think she'd actually accept my help, minor as it was, but then she slid her smaller hand into mine and I released the breath I was holding.

Our eyes met as that little tingling sensation traveled between us. I gave her a little tug, helping her up to standing, and she straightened out the shirt that was plastered to the front of her body.

"I guess I might as well jog on the treadmill since my shirt's already wet," she said wryly.

Like some kind of a pervert, I couldn't tear my eyes away from her wet shirt.

She must have thought I didn't understand her joke because she added, "You know, since running will make me sweat."

I nodded, uncharacteristically tongue-tied around her. "Just try not to have any more catastrophes, will you? I might not be around to help you next time."

Her eyes flashed with annoyance, but she flounced off without another word. I'm not ashamed to admit I was staring at her ass while she walked away. It was a nice one. Unlike most women our age, Amy was still fit and trim. Not that physical appearance was everything of course, but I did like a woman who took care of herself.

As I finished my workout, I kept sneaking looks at Amy but she studiously ignored me. I wasn't sure how I managed to piss her off every time we met, but I needed to break through her prickly exterior and get to know her. After all, we were going to spend the rest of our lives together. She just didn't know it yet.

Amy

"Are you settling in okay?" Julie asked.

We'd agreed to meet for coffee on Saturday morning in the Silver Falls "town square". It was a cute little area that offered a grocery store, a café, an Italian restaurant, a gift shop, and a fabulous coffee shop.

"Yeah, everything is good," I reassured my friend. "Thanks again for letting me move in."

"You're paying rent," she reminded me. "No need to keep thanking me. In fact, if you bring it up again, I'm going to make you pay more. This isn't a thing, Amy. We're family."

"I love you too, Jules," I smiled.

I glanced up as two men walked by wearing shorts, tee shirts, and light jackets. I deduced from the tennis rackets over their shoulders that they were coming from the tennis courts. It was late December, which seemed a bit cold for playing tennis, but the cooler temperatures didn't seem to bother them. They were both attractive older men, one who kind of reminded me of that guy from "Fantasy Island" and one who had a bit of an older Robert Redford look about him.

They both gave me friendly smiles as they walked by, making my heart race the tiniest bit.

"Oh. My. God," I mouthed to Julie.

She laughed. "I know, right? That's why they call this place Silver Fox Falls. I've never seen so many good looking older men in one place before. And Dante swears it's just a coincidence, that they did no special recruitment for studly older guys."

"Wow." I jokingly fanned myself with my hand.

"Not that Dante has noticed the studly older guys," she added. "He didn't even know about the Silver Fox nickname until I explained it to him. Although he can be a bit clueless."

"How is it now that you're officially living there?" I asked. "Are you guys fighting about socks on the floor or the proper way to hang toilet paper?"

Julie got a distinctly non-Julie dreamy look on her face. "No fighting. In fact, it's going great. After both of us living alone for so many years, I honestly expected it to be more difficult to adapt to living together. I guess it helps that we're both pretty easy going and flexible."

"I'm sure that's what Dante loves the most about you," I teased.

"What?" Julie looked confused.

"Your flexibility."

I waggled my eyebrows suggestively to emphasize the joke, and Julie rolled her eyes. "Weirdo."

"I can't even imagine living with someone again after all these years," I said. "I haven't lived with anyone since I broke up with Robert and that was what? Twenty years ago?"

I'd moved into my duplex after that break-up and had lived there alone ever since.

"Yeah, you're definitely set in your ways," Julie agreed. "But Silver Fox Falls is a fresh start for you. I know you said you wanted to meet new people and who knows? Maybe you'll find a special someone too."

An image of Sam flashed across my mind before I ruthlessly pushed it away.

"I doubt that," I said mildly.

"All I'm saying is, don't shut yourself off to possibilities," Julie pressed. "But also, remember if you date anyone here and it doesn't work out, you will be running into them after you break up. All. The. Time. This place is totally like a small town."

"I'll remember that," I promised.

"By the way, have you met your new neighbors yet?" Julie asked. "Everyone on the floor seemed nice but thanks to Dante, I honestly didn't spend enough time at my condo to make any lasting impressions."

"Yeah, I've met some of them," I answered. "Mrs. Lewis next door is a sweetie, even if she is a little wacky. I briefly met the Andersons across the hall. Oh, and I've run into the guy next door a few times too."

"Sam? Yeah, he's a great guy."

"Do you, ah, know him very well?" I asked, striving to be casual.

Julie's eyes narrowed, telling me I hadn't been as cool as I'd attempted to be.

"Not well, no," she said slowly. "We chatted a few times, but I started hooking up with Dante almost as soon as I moved here, so I really only saw Sam a few times."

"Hooking up?" I laughed. "You sound like a kid."

She shrugged. "I think Dante knows him, but other than a 'hi, how are you?' kind of thing I've never really talked to him enough to get a sense of what he's like."

She paused to take a sip of her coffee and I had the sense that she was waiting for me to ask more about Sam. I wasn't going to give her the satisfaction, especially because I definitely did not want to know more about the jerk who kept rescuing me.

For some reason I kept running into him right when I was courting catastrophe. First, he kept me from falling in the hallway. Then I ran into him at the gym after I spilled my water, and I managed to clunk our heads together. And just yesterday I was passing him in the parking lot, and he saved me from tripping over one of those concrete dividers between the rows of parking spots.

Then again, I only tripped because I was distracted at the sight of him walking across the parking lot wearing tight jeans, a leather bomber jacket, and mirror sunglasses. He looked like he'd just walked off the set of *Top Gun* which, in my defense, would have distracted any straight woman with a pulse.

"Do you want me to ask Dante if he's single?" Julie asked.

"God no, I really don't care," I lied.

"Does he wear a wedding ring?" she asked.

"No," I said without thinking.

She pointed at me. "Hah! You do like him! You checked out his ring finger."

I crossed my arms over my chest. "I just happened to notice, is all."

"Yeah sure, you keep telling yourself that," Julie laughed. "And I'll remind you about this conversation at your wedding."

My mouth dropped open. "What happened to you living here? Is there something in the water or something? You've never been one to talk about love and boys and marriage."

"That's because I never knew how great all those things could be until I met Dante."

I sighed softly. "I'm glad you found happiness here Julie, but that doesn't mean I will."

"It doesn't mean you won't either."

Sam

For the next week I managed to run into my new neighbor once or twice a day.

Three or four times I saw her in the hallway in front of our apartments when a client was coming or going from a session. Each time she'd glared at me like she was offended by the women I was helping, which totally confused me.

One day I saw her in the community coffee shop having coffee with her friend Julie. I'd made a point to go over and say hello, although Amy had seemed irritated by my interruption. I'd been flirting my ass off – much to Julie's obvious amusement – and got nowhere.

***

"Ladies," I said smoothly. "How are you both today?"

"Oh, hi there, Sam."

Julie gave me a big smile. She seemed excited to see me, unlike Amy who was just scowling at me.

"Hi Amy. You look pretty today." I pulled out a chair. "Do you mind if I join you two?"

"There's an open table over there." Amy pointed across the room. "Plenty of space."

"The view's better here," I said, giving her a wink. She rolled her eyes like a petulant teenager.

"Amy!" Julie chastised her friend, then turned to me. "How's everything going? How's your family? Did you all have a nice Christmas?"

I could see Amy paying close attention to our conversation, watching me out of the corner of her eye.

"It was nice. My son Paul had a couple of days leave from the military, so we had a huge holiday dinner on Christmas Eve. Then we all got up early to watch the kids open their gifts from Santa."

I had two grown kids with my ex-wife. My son was single still and stationed in South Carolina. My daughter Penny was married with three adorable little girls who had me wrapped around their little fingers.

"They're so cute when they're little and Christmas is still magic for them."

"Yeah, they are," I agreed.

"Do you have kids, Amy?"

She sent me a look I couldn't interpret. "No."

Julie frowned at her again. "Amy's always been like a second mother to my kids though. The two of us have been friends most of our lives, since high school in fact."

"That's great. I went to my high school reunion a few years ago and I didn't know anybody. I kept wondering why there were so many old people at the reunion."

Julie laughed at my joke and when the corner of Amy's mouth quirked, I decided to call it a win.

"Well, it looks like my coffee is ready. I'll let you two get back to your conversation. See you both later."

***

The next day I saw Amy in the shared parking lot between our building and the neighboring one. She hadn't been paying attention to where she was going, and I saved her from tripping over a concrete divider in the parking lot, grabbing her arm just in time to keep her from face planting on the asphalt.

I couldn't help but wonder if Amy was always this clumsy, or if she was as rattled by me as I was by her. I'd noticed her checking me out right before she tripped.

She'd ignored my attempts at conversation, stomping off towards her car like I'd offended her by my mere existence. I was a sick bastard, because the more Amy acted like she hated me, the more determined I became to change her mind.

A few days later I was coming back from running some errands and saw Amy walking ahead of me on the sidewalk that led from the parking lot. I couldn't say why, but even though she was bundled up against the cold and almost half a block ahead of me, I recognized her. Somehow my body knew it was her the instant she came into my sights. Eager to chat with Amy and get to know her better, I quickened my steps, trying to catch up with her.

She was almost to the corner of our building when she slipped on the ice and took a header into a snowbank. Jeez, I really needed to wrap this woman in bubble wrap. She hadn't even seen me this time and still she was having accidents. Gingerly I jogged over to her, offering a hand to help her get up out of the snow.

"Disaster follows you everywhere, huh?" I teased.

Instead of returning my smile, Amy frowned at me. She ignored my hand, trying to get up without my help and just making herself sink more into the soft snowbank. With an impatient sigh, I grabbed her underneath her arms and yanked her up to standing.

"I was fine," she huffed as she brushed the snow off her clothes.

She was wearing an oversized puffy coat that went all the way to her knees, boots, and a wool beanie. I curled my hands into fists to resist pulling her into my arms and kissing that frown off her face.

"Yeah, I could see that," I said with barely concealed amusement. "So, how are you, Amy? Besides wet. Again."

Something flared in her eyes. I'd been referring to the snow that was seeping through her clothes the same way the water had soaked her the other day in the gym, but clearly that wasn't what Amy was thinking about. Following her train of thought, I felt my dick twitch in my pants.

I couldn't explain the draw I felt towards this woman who'd obviously decided not to like me, but it was running through me with an intensity that would have freaked me out if it didn't feel so right. I wasn't sure what I'd done to make her dislike me so much, but I needed to fix this, and fast. Before I could say anything else though, she waved a finger at me.

"I'm fine. But do me a favor, would you? Try to keep the noise down. Other people live in the building too, you know."

I reeled a little from the change in topic. "What are you talking about?"

"Your music. It was way too freaking loud last night. And I hate the Rolling Stones."

I liked to listen to music when I was cooking or doing things around the house, but I didn't think it was that loud. Then again, I'd lost some of my hearing as I'd aged. Julie had never mentioned the noise, although she'd fallen for Dante not that long after she moved in, so she hadn't spent a lot of time in her apartment from what I could tell. Or maybe my music was fine with her and that's why she hadn't said anything. Either way, I made a mental note to keep the music down.

"My apologies," I said smoothly. "I'm partially deaf in one ear so I'm not always aware of how loud things are. I'll try to watch the volume in the future."

"Yeah, do that."

She turned and walked away without another word. I followed her like a puppy.

Amy

I winced at the shrewish tone in my voice. I felt completely amped up from this short encounter. Meanwhile, Sam was completely unruffled, watching me like he was trying to figure me out. When I spun around and stalked back to my apartment, Sam was on my heels the entire time.

We got into the elevator, each of us retreating to our sides of the small space, although I could feel Sam's eyes on mine the entire short ride. The doors opened and we headed into the atrium area that each floor had. There was a young woman standing there wearing skinny jeans that looked like they were painted on, a sweater that was at least two sizes too small, and high heeled boots that were way too flimsy for the snowfall we'd gotten last night.

"Hi Sam," she said, her voice soft and breathy.

"Good afternoon, Mary, my apologies for running late." He sent a quick look in my direction. "I was helping a neighbor."

I stomped down to my apartment, unsure why I was so irritated. Oh yeah, maybe because every time I saw this man I was making a fool of myself? Although it wasn't Sam's fault that I was clumsy and kept needing rescuing.

The truth was I was also irrationally annoyed by the steady stream of cute young girls who came to Sam's apartment every day. Why were they there? Were they all his girlfriends? Were they prostitutes? Was he filming porn next door? I'd seen at least six different women go over there over the last week. It didn't make any sense.

It was more than that though. I mean, the girls were bad enough, but there was something else about Sam. He made me feel...unsettled. I didn't like feeling unsettled.

I also didn't like being rude, and the truth was, I'd been super rude to him, especially after he helped me get out of the snow drift. It wasn't like me at all. I was usually a pretty cheerful person, the kind of person who went out of their way to be nice to people. This new version of me wasn't nice and wasn't likable.

I was ashamed of how I'd been acting towards Sam. I really needed to apologize.

My job as a controller for a large organization had been on a hybrid schedule ever since the pandemic. Usually, I went into the office two days a week and worked from home for three, but this morning I'd gone into the office for an in-person meeting. I was coming back home from the meeting when I ran into Sam.

And he'd rescued me once again.

After changing into dry clothes, I booted up my laptop to finish out my workday, losing myself in the world of numbers and spreadsheets. I could figure out what to do about my neighbor after I was off the clock.

By the time I finished work a few hours later I'd decided that the simplest thing to do would be to go over and apologize. I briefly considered baking him cookies or something, but then I remembered I sucked at baking. I didn't want to make things any worse with Sam.

Emptyhanded, I headed next door. I raised my hand to knock, but the door opened before my fingers connected with the wood.

"Oh. Hi."

I looked between Sam and yet another woman, this one a little older, dressed in baggy clothes that swallowed her small frame. She gave me a curious look before saying goodbye to Sam and heading down the hallway. I watched her walk to the elevator, trying to figure out what the hell was going on here.

There was only one way to find out. Ask. Of course, technically it wasn't my business.

"Is she one of your girlfriends?"

Sam laughed. "No, she's a client."

"You're a gigolo?" My mouth dropped in shock.

Sam looked at me like I was nuts.

"What? No. I'm a financial counselor."

"What kind of financial counselor?" I asked.

"I offer personalized financial empowerment work. I specialize in helping women who are suddenly on their own due to divorce or widowhood," Sam explained. "I work with them to develop budgets, set up a savings plan, create a retirement strategy, things like that. It's something I started doing after I retired from the for-profit financial services company I used to work at."

Hmm. That sounded kind of noble. But still...

"You do this work in your home?" I asked suspiciously.

He nodded. "I've created a separate office area in my apartment, and I got permission from the homeowners association to operate a business in this space as long as it doesn't disturb the neighbors," he said. "Do you want to come in and see my office?"

I so did.

Following Sam, I noted that his apartment was larger than my little one bedroom. I remembered Julie mentioning that this building was a mix of one and two bedroom units.

He had put up a wall at one end of the large entryway. It wasn't a full wall, it went up maybe seven feet, leaving a few feet of space between the wall and the ceiling, which let some light through but effectively separated the living space from the office. A closed door was located in the center, with watercolor prints on either side of the door. To the right there was a small room that I assumed was originally a guest bedroom and a half bath. To the left there was a narrow door that I assumed led to a closet.

"Nice set up," I said, impressed. It looked like a normal office lobby.

I decided to check out the office. It was painted a light blue color which brightened up the windowless space, and more artwork on the walls, these depicting calming outdoor scenes.

The office had a standard sized desk, several books, a computer, and one of those large screens that looked like a TV but was really a computer monitor. I had one of those in my office as well. Excel was open on the screen, open to a spreadsheet with what looked like household expenses. It was definitely a budget.

Sam was quiet as I poked around his office. I replayed his explanation in my head.

"You only work with women?" I asked, turning around and planting my ass against the corner of his desk.

He shook his head. "No, I *specialize* in working with women. Most of my clients are women because I do pro bono work for the domestic violence shelter. I also get referrals from divorce lawyers and grief support groups for paid clients, and I offer a sliding scale rate for lower income women."

"Why?"

"Why what?" he hedged.

"Why do you specialize in working with women?"

It wasn't my business, but I wanted to know. Sam's face closed off a little, and when he spoke again, his voice was carefully neutral.

"There's a history of domestic violence in my family. I saw firsthand how women are placed in situations where they can't leave bad relationships because they're too scared about handling money. Financial control is a big component of domestic violence," he explained. "After making a lot of money helping rich people get richer, I wanted to give back to women who need a little assistance getting on their feet."

I had the strangest urge to pull him into a hug, but instead I pressed my fingers against the edge of the desk on either side of my hips. Sam had been attractive when I thought he was a philandering asshole. Now that I knew he was a good guy, I was about five minutes from falling in love with him.

"I'm sorry I misjudged you," I said quietly. "I thought you were...well, I wasn't sure what the hell was happening here with so many different women coming in and out. But I also wanted to apologize for being rude to you outside. I'm not normally a rude person."

"Only with me?" he asked.

His tone was teasing but the way he brushed his palm down his shirt seemed more about nerves than pressing out wrinkles.

"There is something about you that's super annoying," I said teasingly, trying to lighten the mood. "But I really am sorry. There's no excuse for my bad behavior. I hope you'll forgive me."

"Maybe we should…"

Whatever Sam was going to say was cut off by a knock on the door.

"That's my next client," he said regretfully.

I nodded, pushing off the desk and heading towards the door.

"See you around, neighbor," I said, striving for a casual tone despite the confused feelings I was experiencing right now.

I couldn't help the little thrill I felt when he called after me, "I hope so, Amy."

Sam

"Have you met Amy yet?" Dante asked.

We'd gotten to the gym at the same time this morning and were jogging next to each other on the treadmills so we could catch. It was way too freaking cold to run outside. I liked Dante. We weren't friends or anything, but we'd worked out together a few times and talked at Silver Falls community events. Today I had an ulterior motive though: I was hoping to get some intel on Amy.

I'd been to the gym every single morning since the time I ran into Amy here, but I hadn't seen her come in again. I wasn't sure if it was because she'd already given up on her fitness plan or if she was trying to avoid running into me again here. Since we'd cleared the air two days ago I was hoping she'd be back, but I hadn't seen her since she left my apartment.

"Oh yeah, I've met Amy."

Dante's gaze swung to mine before returning to the front of his machine. "Sounds like there's a story there."

I blew out a breath.

"She's...well, there's something about her. I've never met anyone like her, but she kind of hates me. Although that might have been because she thought I was a gigolo."

It still made me chuckle that she'd thought I was a gigolo. Who would think something like that?

Dante tripped on the treadmill, then grabbed the handles and reduced his speed to a fast walk. I followed suit, grabbing my water bottle and taking a long drink.

"Why did she think you're a gigolo exactly?" Dante asked, laughter in his voice.

"She saw women coming in and out of my apartment and that's where her mind went I guess."

I rolled my lips in. It was funny really, except that I'd fallen in love at first sight with a woman who thought that little of me.

"You cleared it all up, I assume?" Dante asked.

"Yeah, but I'm pretty sure she's avoiding me." I couldn't help the glum tone in my voice.

"Why do you think that?"

"Just an instinct," I said.

"You like her," Dante said. It was a statement, not a question.

"Yeah. Let me ask you something," I said, turning the treadmill off so I could see Dante's face when he responded. "What was it like when you met Julie?"

Dante stopped walking and got a sappy look on his face.

"At my age, I figured all that romantic crap was just made up, you know? But the instant I saw Julie, I felt this kind of jolt, like my heart was restarting or something. I had the strangest feeling like I'd just found something that I didn't even know was lost, some part of me that was missing until I met her."

He shook his head. "I know it sounds weird, but that's how it was."

"No, I get it, because that's exactly what happened for me. The first time I saw Amy I was keeping her from falling..."

"Oh yeah, that woman is quite the klutz."

"I touched her, and even though I hadn't seen her face yet, I just knew. I knew she was the woman for me," I explained. "But unfortunately, I seem to fluster her. When I'm not pissing her off that is. I'm pretty sure she hates me."

"You don't know that. I thought Julie hated me at first. And well, she did. But no woman hates a man that much without there being something else there." Dante snapped his fingers. "What are you doing tonight?"

"I have clients until six, then nothing."

"How about you come over for dinner when you get done. Amy will be there, and it'll give you a chance to get to know each other with me and Julie as a buffer."

"Are you sure Julie won't mind?"

"Nah, she'll be thrilled," Dante said. "She's been wanting to fix Amy up with someone anyway."

Later that day I knocked on Dante's door with a mix of nervousness and excitement. Julie answered the door, taking the bottle of wine from my hand and pulling me in for a big hug.

"Sam! It's so nice to see you."

She pulled back and gave me a meaningful look that I interpreted to mean that Dante had told her about my predicament with her best friend. Of course, she'd probably figured it out when we all had coffee and I'd been staring at her friend like a lovesick puppy.

I stepped into the spacious penthouse. It took up the entire floor and had incredible views of the city. I greeted Dante with a handshake before turning to greet Amy. She was looking between me and Julie suspiciously.

"Hi Amy, it's nice to see you again," I said politely.

"Hi Sam, this is a surprise." She slightly emphasized the word *surprise* then shot another look at Julie.

At least she wasn't glaring at me, that was a definite step up from the other times we'd run into each other.

"Dinner's just about ready," Julie said brightly. "Why don't you two sit down and I'll help Dante bring out dinner?"

Amy and I sat across from each other. The small square table was set up with a tablecloth, napkins, and nicer dishes than I used on a regular basis.

Seeing me study the obviously expensive plates, Amy said, "Yeah, I'm wondering what's with the fine china too. Last time I was here we ate off of Julie's Ikea plates."

I met her eyes, both of us smiling, and our gazes stayed locked for a long, breathless moment. I could practically feel the air between us heating. At this stage in my life, I thought strong passion, that sense of 'I need to touch this woman right now', was past. But staring into Amy's dark blue eyes, my cock rising to half mast just from a look, and I knew that part of my life was far from over. It was just the beginning.

Julie hustled in, Dante on her heels, and we looked away from each other. Amy ran her fingers through her spiky hair nervously, then took a deep breath. I was glad to see that I'd affected her as much as she affected me.

"What's for dinner?" she asked.

We all looked at Dante. Everyone knew the man was a gourmet cook. His fiancée hated cooking, so they were a good match. He cooked, and she ate.

"I made Greek lemon chicken, with orzo, asparagus, sauteed mushrooms, and a Greek salad. Oh, and I baked some bread too."

My mouth watered just hearing about it. I was a decent enough cook, but the truth was I didn't really like it that much, especially when I was just cooking for one. I had cereal or microwave burritos for dinner more times than I'd like to admit.

"You've got yourself a keeper, Jules," Amy teased her friend.

Julie leaned over and pressed a quick kiss to Dante's cheek. "Don't I know it."

Dinner was delicious and we all chatted easily, although I couldn't help but sneak quick looks at Amy. I knew that Dante had invited me over here to help set me up with Amy and it appeared that her friend Julie was on board too because she spent most of the meal talking us up.

"Amy, did you know that Sam helps women leaving bad marriages?" Julie asked.

"Yes, I did know that." Amy and I exchanged a long, heated look. "He explained about his work the other day."

"Well Sam, did you know that Amy manages the entire financial department at her job? She's a controller."

"No, I didn't," I responded, my eyes still on Amy. "It's funny that we both work with numbers."

"Yeah."

Amy was different tonight. Without radiating hostility and encasing herself in a protective shell she was softer. Gentler. Maybe it was the two glasses of wine she'd drank, but I was hoping it was that she was finally warming up to me.

Amy

"And the best news of all?" Julie said brightly. "You're both single. Isn't that great?"

My eyes shot over to Julie's as her matchmaking turned from subtle to overt. I was so going to talk to her about this later. She knew how much I hated being fixed up, blind dates especially. I had no idea that Sam would be here tonight until he knocked on the door. Not that I was totally opposed to learning more about him, now that I knew he wasn't exploiting women next door to me.

"Julie," I said warningly. "What are you doing?"

She gave me a look of faux innocence. "Just making conversation, Ames."

I shook my head at Julie's over the top matchmaking attempts. Across the table, Dante seemed to be trying not to laugh.

"Yeah Jules, we get the message," I teased. "You're hoping to fix us up."

"Is it working?" Julie asked, not missing a beat.

My eyes flew to Sam, who gave me a flirty smile, and the room suddenly felt a little too warm.

"Let's talk about the wedding," I suggested, desperate to redirect her before I did something stupid like leap across the table and rip off Sam's clothes. "Did you two decide on a venue yet?"

I breathed a sigh of relief as the conversation turned back to Julie and Dante. We finished dinner, then the four of us shared another bottle of wine in the living room, looking out through the large picture windows that overlooked the entire Silver Falls community. Dante had been the developer of this community and as part of that, he'd built himself the largest and highest place in the neighborhood. The view was incredible. In the distance you could see the lights of Denver.

I would hate him, but the truth was even though he was disgustingly rich he wasn't pretentious or showy. He acted like an average guy and, most importantly, he treated my best friend like a freaking queen. After standing by while she navigated a shitty marriage and a long stint as a single mom, I loved that she was finally focused on herself. Finding love with a great guy was just a bonus.

Glancing at Sam out of the corner of my eye, I wondered what it would be like to be that much in love. I'd never been in love before, not really, but I felt drawn to Sam in a way I hadn't experienced before. It felt like way more than simple attraction. Could it be love?

I pushed the thought out of my mind. That was ridiculous. I didn't even know this guy. Maybe I should just sleep with him and get him out of my system. But then again, what if I did that and he got attached? Or what if I got attached?

"I'd better head home," I said, pushing to my feet. "I have to work in the morning. Thanks for a great evening. Dinner was delicious, Dante."

Sam stood up as well. "I'll walk you home."

"That's not necessary," I protested automatically.

"We live next door to each other and we're both leaving right now," Sam pointed out. "Should I just walk a half a block behind you or something?"

Well, when he put it like that, I was being ridiculous. After giving Julie and Dante a hug, I bundled up in my coat, scarf and mittens and headed out of the building with Sam on my side. I inhaled deeply, filling my lungs with cold, clean air.

"Sorry about all the matchmaking stuff with Julie," I said after several moments of silence.

It was cold outside, the kind of cold where it made your face hurt, and we were both walking quickly to get out of the elements. Fortunately, we only lived a short distance from Dante's building. The sky was dark, but lights clearly illuminated the path between our buildings. The sidewalks were cleared from yesterday's snowstorm, although huge piles of snow lined the perimeter.

Sam pulled the lobby door open for me and I ducked under his arm, sighing as I felt the warmth of the building penetrate my thick layers of clothing.

"Jeez it's cold out there," I announced unnecessarily as I unzipped my coat and shoved my scarf and mittens into the pocket.

"Yeah."

Sam pressed the button for the elevator, and we stood in silence until the doors opened, admitting us into the small space. Then, it was like someone had fired a starter pistol or something because we flew together, meeting in the middle of the space. Sam's palms came up to cup my cheeks and I wrapped my arms around him, pulling him close as his lips crashed down on mine.

Oh my God. I'd never felt so instantly aroused in my life.

Sam spun me around until my back was pressed against the wall of the elevator, the little handrail pressing against my lower back. Not that I cared. The only thing I cared about right now was sucking his tongue into my mouth and deepening the kiss.

Dimly I heard the elevator ding, but when we kept on kissing, the doors slid shut again.

I widened my stance, rolling my pelvis against the leg that Sam shoved between my thighs. I ground against him shamelessly as the kiss went on and on. My entire body was burning up, and I wondered if he could feel how wet I was even between layers of clothes.

The elevator dinged again, and this time when the doors opened, we were on a different floor. I heard a loud, outraged gasp. The two of us pulled apart, leaning against the walls, panting for breath as an elderly woman came inside with an ugly dog and a judgmental look on her face.

"My grandchildren visit me here, you know," she sniffed.

"Sorry ma'am, mine do too. We got a little carried away."

Sam's attempts to charm her did little to improve her mood. We rode down to the lobby, the air heavy with the weight of her disapproval, and after she exited, Sam pressed the button for our floor again. This time we stayed in our respective corners, both lost in thought.

I felt Sam's eyes on me and when I looked, I realized that I was tracing my lips with my fingers. They were swollen from our passionate kisses. I had a feeling that no matter what happened next, I'd be reliving this kiss for quite a while.

We walked outside the elevator, side by side as we made our way up the hallway. My mind was racing, simultaneously confused and excited by what had just happened. I mean, I knew I was attracted to this guy, but I had no idea I was *that* attracted to him.

I'd never completely lost myself in a kiss before. If Sam could bring me that much pleasure with a kiss, what could he do with actual sex? I was determined to find out.

"Would you like to come in?" I asked as we approached my front door.

It took him longer to answer than I would have expected.

"I'd better not."

I stopped dead, my mouth opening in shock. Honestly, I thought that was just a pro forma question. After what had happened in the elevator, how was rejecting what he must know was a sure thing?

"I thought we could continue what we started in the elevator," I said, giving him a bold look.

"It's late, we should probably go our separate ways."

He almost looked panicky as he stared over my shoulder like he was plotting his escape to the door down the hall.

"It's only nine o'clock!"

It wasn't like me to cajole, but I still couldn't believe this was happening. Not to be vain, but I'd always been good looking and fit, and I couldn't remember one single time a man had rejected me in my entire life. What the hell?

He continued to avoid my gaze, his chest heaving. His muscles looked coiled for flight.

"Okay, fine," I said, striving to keep the hurt out of my voice. "I guess, I guess I'll see you around then."

I shoved my key in the lock and opened my door, stepping quickly inside.

"Amy. Wait."

"Good night."

I slammed the door in his face.

When Julie texted me later that night to ask how things had gone with Sam, I didn't bother to answer.

Sam

I stared up at the ceiling in the darkness, calling myself every name in the book. I'd choked. I'd quite literally had Amy in my hands – or her ass anyway – and instead of taking her up on the offer to go inside her apartment and fuck her until her eyes rolled back in her head, I'd said no.

She'd probably never talk to me now and even if she did, I had no clue how I'd even explain it. How did you tell a woman you'd just met a week ago that you'd fallen in love with her the minute you laid eyes on her and while you'd wanted nothing more in this world than to make love to her, you'd psyched yourself out?

Things had been fine when we were making out. More than fine. Kissing Amy had been electric. Life changing. And that was the problem. We'd been in the elevator with that judgmental old lady and her yippy little dog, and my mind had started racing with 'what ifs'.

What if I was in love with her but she just wanted me for a quick roll in the hay? What if she broke my heart? What if I didn't get her off? Or worse yet, what if I had performance issues? It had never happened before but at my age, things sometimes didn't work properly. What if I did something stupid like shout out that I loved her during sex?

For the first time in a long time, I'd succumbed to the anxiety that used to plague me when I was younger. Desperate to get away from Amy before I did something embarrassing like hyperventilate, I'd practically sprinted away from her.

Once I'd gotten inside, I'd slid to the floor of my apartment and done breathing exercises until I felt the anxiety recede, but by then it was too late to return to Amy's house.

How could I ever fix this?

Despite the cold temperatures I decided to run outside the next morning, desperate for a long, hard run that would make my mind focus. Running outside was much better than a treadmill, it allowed me to fully relax into my thoughts. I'd solved a lot of problems while running, and I was hoping that lightning would strike again.

Sadly it didn't. When I returned from my run, lungs heaving and legs burning, I was no closer to figuring out how to fix things with Amy.

I was too embarrassed to ask Dante for help, so I decided I'd wait until the next time I ran into Amy and hope for divine intervention. It was a stupid plan, but it was all I had.

Despite the fact that we'd run into each other at least once a day the previous two weeks, we managed to not see each other for three days. With every passing day, I grew more nervous about it. Was she avoiding me now?

I thought I was doing a pretty good job of hiding my emotional turmoil until Friday night. I was invited over to my daughter's house for a family dinner. Penny lived in the suburbs with her wife Monica and her three kids from Penny's first marriage.

Honestly, I couldn't say I was surprised when my daughter came out as a lesbian. Her mother and I had always suspected as much, at least until she got married to a man and started popping out kids. Turns out we'd been right all along.

Now Penny was happily married and hosting big, blended family dinners once a month. Usually I looked forward to seeing everyone, but tonight I wasn't in the right headspace for family dynamics.

Jane and I had been married for about ten years, then had an amicable divorce, co-parenting Penny and our son Paul with more ease than most divorced couples. It helped that we'd been friends before we got married and stayed friends after. Ours hadn't been a love match and we'd known that going in. We were two friends who'd given up on finding love and decided to make a life together.

When she met her now-husband Mark, Jane had been honest about her feelings from the start. While I'd never expected to be divorced, I was happy that Jane found Mark. She'd found something with him that we'd never had: passion. And now that I'd met Amy, I understood this even more.

"You." Jane pointed at me as soon as the dinner plates were cleared. "Come with me. We need to talk."

Penny, Monica, and Mark all looked up in surprise at Jane's firm words. My ex-wife was generally soft-spoken unless she was in her mama bear mode. Jane strode into the guest room, assuming that I'd follow her, which of course I did.

"What's wrong with you?" she asked without preamble as she closed the door. "You've been mostly MIA the last couple of weeks, barely responding to my texts, and tonight you look like someone killed your puppy."

I guessed Jane had noticed that I hadn't been returning her texts like usual. I wasn't sure why, other than I'd been spending all of my non-working time obsessing over Amy like a teenaged boy with a crush on his teacher. Or maybe I just wasn't ready to talk about it until now.

"I'm in love."

No sense in prevaricating. Jane would get the truth out of me anyway. She was a master interrogator. She reared back in surprise.

"Why don't you look happy about that?" she asked. "You always wanted to find true love. And who is this woman, anyway? How did you meet her?"

"Her name is Amy. We met about three weeks ago when she moved in next door. Unfortunately, she hates me. At least I'm pretty sure she does."

"What did you do?" Jane asked.

I told her the whole story, from Amy thinking I was a gigolo to my freaking out when we'd finally kissed after having dinner with Dante and Julie.

"I'd finally got her to warm up to me—."

"More than warm up, it sounds like," Jane interrupted teasingly.

"And now I messed it all up again," I continued.

"This was, when?"

"Three days ago."

We were sitting across from each other on the bed, and Jane reached across to smack me on the side of the head.

"Why haven't you contacted her since then, you idiot? You don't reject a woman and then let her stew about it for three damned days! That's a long time for a woman who probably thinks that you rejected her to ruminate on what an asshole you are."

"I didn't know what to say," I admitted. "I figured I'd just wait until I ran into her, and then inspiration would strike, but I haven't seen her since that night, which is weird because usually I run into her once or twice a day."

"She's probably avoiding you, genius." Jane and I knew each other too well to pull punches.

"Yeah," I said miserably. "I'm sure she is."

"I haven't seen you be this anxious since Penny got married, and I've never seen you get anxious about a woman," Jane noted. "You need to get out of your head and just talk to her. Soon."

"But what do I say?"

"Tell her the truth. The kiss was so incredible it freaked you out, and because you're a processor, you needed some time to process what happened before doing something more." Jane said. "Tell her that you sometimes struggle with anxiety in new or challenging situations."

"I don't want to sound like a pussy," I said quietly.

"First of all, you and I both know that anxiety is a medical condition," she said firmly. "Secondly, most women would be thrilled to have a guy who actually analyzes their feelings, trust me on this. But if she has a bad reaction, she's probably not the woman for you, and then you'll know it's not going to work."

"She is the woman for me," I said firmly.

"Then you're going to need to man up and go talk to her," Jane said. "Whatever she's thinking happened between you two is probably way worse than the truth is."

When I didn't respond, Jane continued.

"You are a great guy, Sam. You deserve love. And if this woman is half as awesome as you think she is, you two have the chance to create something good together. I want that for you."

She pulled me into a tight hug. "Now get the hell out of here and go apologize to your girl."

Amy

I frowned as I heard someone knocking on the front door. It was just after nine-thirty, way too late for a random drop-in from anyone. Silver Falls was a gated community with secured entrances at every building, so whoever this was, they lived here.

Figuring it was probably Julie, I didn't bother to find a robe, opening the door in my sleeping pants and a threadbare sweatshirt. To my surprise, Sam stood in the hallway, dressed neatly in pressed khaki pants, a button down shirt, and loafers.

"Are you here to sell me insurance?" I asked.

He frowned. "What?"

I gestured to his outfit. "You're dressed kind of professional for nine-thirty on a Friday night."

"Oh. No. I had a family dinner. With my family."

He seemed oddly nervous, looking everywhere but at me. I didn't understand why his personality seemed to have changed once we kissed. It was weird.

"Did you need something?" I finally asked.

"Could we talk?"

I hesitated, torn between wanting to know what he wanted to talk about, and telling myself I didn't care.

"Please. I promise I'll leave if you ask me to, but there's something I want to talk about with you. It's important."

Well, that was intriguing.

"Fine." I opened the door further to let him. "Come on in. I was just about to make some tea."

I gestured for him to sit at the postage stamp sized table in the kitchen while I put the tea kettle on. I found two cups, putting them on a table with a large box filled with different varieties of tea.

"Wow, you must like tea," he said, using his pointer finger to flip through his tea bag options.

I didn't answer. When the kettle boiled I poured us each some water, then slid into a chair across from Sam. Steam rose between us as we steeped our tea.

"What did you want to talk about?" I finally asked, the curiosity getting the best of me.

While I waited, I studied him carefully, taking in his handsome face, the faint lines around his eyes and the silver in his hair somehow making him even more attractive.

"The other night," he started. "I wanted to come inside you more than anything."

My mouth dropped and his face reddened as he realized what he'd just said. It was adorable. I rolled my lips in to keep from laughing.

"I mean I wanted to come inside *with* you," he clarified. "*With*!"

He shook his head, and I imagined him chastising himself mentally.

"What was stopping you?" I asked, the same question I'd asked myself about a million times since I'd slammed the door in his face the other night. "I wanted the same thing, and I think my signals were pretty clear."

"When I was a younger man, I struggled with anxiety. I'd always had periods of anxiousness, but then I started getting full blown anxiety attacks. They started when I got married and my wife – ex-wife now – got pregnant. The responsibility, it messed with my head."

He paused to swish his tea bag a few times, staring into his cup.

"Twice I went to the ER thinking I was having a heart attack, and both times they told me it was an anxiety attack. I uh, I didn't want to admit it, because anxiety isn't exactly manly, but finally my wife forced me to consider going to therapy. I learned some breathing techniques and went on the meds they were offering me for a while and gradually it got better. In fact, it's been years since I had a full-on anxiety attack."

He took a long sip of his Darjeeling. "When you asked me to come inside with you the other night, I felt a tightening in my chest and suddenly I couldn't breathe, which is how an anxiety attack usually starts for me. So I, well you know, I went home so I wouldn't embarrass myself in front of you."

"Why would I make you anxious?" I asked. "I don't understand."

Sam reached across the table and took my hand in his. Warmth spread wherever our skin touched.

"It's been a while since I've been with a woman," he started. "Things with you are...intense and suddenly everything seemed to be happening too fast. We went from you hating me to you humping my leg in the space of an evening."

Now it was my turn to blush as I remembered my behavior in the elevator. I'd replayed that scene in my head a hundred times since it happened.

"I know I should be coy, but we're too damned old to play games."

He paused again, his eyes bouncing between mine.

"I like you, Amy, I like you in a way that I've never liked anyone before. I don't want to scare you off but what I feel for you, it's big, which made me even more nervous about messing things up with you."

I tried to pull my hand away, but he held on tight.

"You don't even know me enough to like me," I reminded him, but it was a feeble argument. I knew exactly what he was saying, because I felt the same way. Whatever was happening between us went way past simple attraction. It's part of why I'd instinctively pushed him away.

"I want to know you, but I also know I fucked everything up, so my ex-wife said I needed to get my head out of my ass and talk to you," he explained. "That's why I showed up unannounced at nine-thirty on a Friday night."

I frowned as his words registered. "You talked to your ex about me?"

"She's my best friend."

"You're a weird guy, aren't you?" I asked.

"You have no idea." He took a long pause. "I'd like us to..."

Have sex now, I said mentally. I'd been wound tight ever since our make-out session the other night, and no amount of time spent with my battery operated toys was making a dent.

"Go out on a date."

"I don't know," I said teasingly. "I feel like we're going to need to make out some more to make sure it's going to work before I commit to putting you on my very busy social calendar."

Now that I knew I wasn't imagining the red hot attraction between us, I was not going to be coy. Sam smirked and I could practically feel the tension leaving him.

I stood up, then grabbed his wrist, pulling him to stand.

"Enough talking. Enough thinking," I said firmly. "Just kiss me."

Sam

Well, that conversation went better than I'd expected. I'd thought there might be a lot of questions, maybe a laughing comment about anxiety being all in my head, but instead Amy had just accepted what I said at face value. I was incredibly relieved.

"Just kiss me."

She didn't have to ask me twice. I pulled Amy into my arms, pressing our bodies together as I captured her mouth with mine. My tongue slid into her mouth, exploring, and Amy lifted her hands to tunnel into my hair, holding my head close. Immediately every nerve in my body seemed to light up.

I wasn't conscious of the fact that I was walking her backwards until her hips made contact with the counter. I didn't hesitate to boost Amy up and push my way between her thighs. She was a tiny little thing, short and slim, but still soft and curvy.

And strong, I realized as she tightened her legs around my hips and locked her feet behind my upper thighs.

"Jesus," she gasped as we pulled apart.

We were both breathing heavily but my breath stuttered to a stop as she grabbed the hem of the ratty old sweatshirt she was wearing and pulled it over her head, revealing her full breasts.

When I just stared she joked, "They're not as high as they used to be, but they still work for me."

Her breasts were round with dark pink nipples that seemed to point right at me. I couldn't resist lowering my mouth to take a taste. I sucked one pert nipple between my lips, teasing it with my tongue until Amy was arching her back and shoving more of her breast into my mouth. After I gave it a good amount of attention I pulled back, then gave the same treatment to the other breast.

Somehow Amy managed to unbutton my shirt while I was paying homage to her breasts and as soon as I straightened up again, she shoved my shirt over my shoulders. I let it drop to the floor, then pulled my undershirt off, tossing it behind me.

I didn't have the firm, hard body I'd had in my youth, but I still had some muscle definition in my chest and arms despite the softness around my belly.

Her tiny hands massaged up my stomach to circle my pecs and then slid downward again, this time heading for my belt. She paused with her hands on the buckle.

"I want you, Sam," she said. "Just to get this out of the way, I can't get pregnant. And I haven't slept with anyone since my last check-up."

I appreciated her bringing this up, since birth control and testing was the very last thing on my mind right now.

"I'm clean too," I told her. "And I want you more than I want my next breath."

We collided with the energy of horny teenagers. Amy ran her hands up and down my back, scratching me lightly with her nails, while I gripped her ass with one hand and protected her head from banging against the cabinet with the other. I dominated her mouth, sliding my tongue against hers and staking my claim.

Amy's hands slid back towards my waist, and I registered the sound of my zipper opening at the same time that my pants dropped towards my knees. I let her go long enough to shove down my boxers and release my cock, kicking them away so I wouldn't ruin the moment by doing something stupid like tripping on my own pants.

As soon as she saw my cock, Amy smiled.

"I want," she said, making grabby hands towards my crotch.

I couldn't help but laugh.

"Should we go to the bedroom?" I asked reluctantly, not wanting to break the mood.

Amy shimmied out of her pajama pants and kicked them away. "God no, this is way hotter."

I wondered if she was also nervous about ruining the mood. Then her hands were gripping my cock, and I couldn't focus on anything else but this moment with this woman.

Amy lined my cock up with her opening, her legs wrapped back around me, and slowly pulled me closer. The tip breached her opening, and my eyes flew up to hers, partly to make sure it was okay and partly because I wanted the connection.

I slid forward slowly, not stopping until I was fully seated inside her. She felt incredibly tight. My eyes dropped to the place where we were connected, and I moved my hands to grip her naked hips.

"Are you ready?" I whispered.

"God yeah," she said fervently. "Move."

I slid part of the way out, then snapped my hips forward, making Amy groan. And then I did it again a few more times, alternating between slow and fast to heighten our pleasure.

"Faster," she ordered impatiently, her fingernails digging into my shoulders.

I leaned forward and kissed Amy deeply, speeding up the rhythm of my hips to match the way I was sliding my tongue against hers. Her inner muscles squeezed me tight, bringing me closer and closer to orgasm.

There was no way I was going to not let her come first though. I slid one hand between us, exploring her folds until I found the swollen bundle of nerves at her apex. I rolled her clit between my fingers as I continued to thrust in and out, my movements becoming rougher and more erratic.

Suddenly desperate to mark her, I lowered my mouth to the juncture of her shoulder, catching her skin between my teeth and biting down. I hadn't given a woman a hickey since I was in college but damned if I wasn't doing it right now.

Amy stiffened for just an instant, then her body rocked in my arms, her inner muscles squeezing me tight as she found her release. I felt a rush of primal pleasure as she called out my name.

"Sam!"

Hearing my name on her lips and feeling her tightening around me triggered my own orgasm. I felt the telltale sensation of electricity running down my spine, then my balls drew up and I plunged in as deep as I could, painting her womb with spurt after spurt of my cum.

She sagged forward, resting her head on my shoulder as I emptied myself inside her warm pussy. I moved to grip the counter on either side of her hips as my knees threatened to buckle with the force of my orgasm.

When I finally pulled back, empty and depleted, I felt shellshocked.

"Holy shit," Amy whispered, her eyes meeting mine.

"Yeah, holy shit."

I leaned forward to give her another kiss, this one a chaste peck on the lips. I knew I should say something else, but my mind was blissfully blank, my anxiety completely gone.

Fortunately, Amy came to the rescue. She gave me a smile that could only be described as filthy as she grabbed my hand and tugged me away from the counter.

"Let's get some water and try that again in a bed this time."

Amy

I woke up to the most delicious sensation: Sam burrowing under the sheet and sliding in between my legs. I flipped the sheet off of us and saw a long length of naked man. Oh good, last night wasn't just a dream.

"Whatcha doing down there?" I asked with what I hoped was a sexy smile. It was still early in the morning, and we hadn't exactly gotten a lot of sleep last night, what with all the sex.

"I was laying here thinking about how I was too busy fucking you to get a taste of this sweet little pussy," he said.

It should have sounded corny, but somehow it wasn't. That's how far gone I was for this guy already. Maybe I was still drunk from all the orgasms, but last night had been the best night of my life.

I felt the scratch of his beard between my thighs, then his tongue slid in between my lower lips, licking up inside my channel. I made a high pitched noise as my hips levitated off the mattress.

"Oh."

It was all I could come up with at the moment. My brain was short circuiting, all my attention focused on what was happening between my legs.

I reached down to grab his hair, directed him where I wanted him the most, but he lightly smacked my hand away.

"Put your hands over your head," he ordered. "And keep them there."

"Or what?" I asked teasingly.

"Or I'll tie you to the bedframe."

A rush of moisture flooded my core, and I could tell by his satisfied smirk that he'd noticed.

"This is a platform bed," I said in a bratty tone. "But I'll comply since you're being so generous this morning."

His eyes blazed as I shifted my hands underneath my head, the movement arching my back slightly and putting my breasts on display.

"Good girl."

"How about you be a good boy and get back to work?" I said, nodding towards my vag.

Sam flattened his tongue, lapping up the evidence of my increasing arousal, then slipped his tongue inside my channel, pushing in and out while he teased my clit with his fingers. He might have woken me up from a dead sleep, but it didn't take long for me to go right over the edge.

As I rode the waves of my orgasm, I was gripping his head with my thighs so tightly I wondered how I didn't crack his skull. Sam licked and teased me until I finally sagged against the mattress, fully sated.

Then he crawled back up my body, pulled the discarded blanket back over us, and cuddled me to his side.

This wasn't me. I wasn't a cuddler. I almost never had guys sleep over, much preferring to stay at their house so I could leave whenever I wanted. But waking up with Sam, it felt different. It felt right.

And I wasn't prepared to analyze why that was...

The next time I woke up, I was ravenously hungry. Sam headed over to his place to take a shower while I cleaned up here, then we met in the hallway and walked hand in hand down to the café for breakfast.

I was glad that Sam trusted me enough to tell me about his anxiety last night. We'd talked more as we laid in bed together, sated from our second round of lovemaking, and it was clear to me that it was hard for him to talk about it. I got it, guys in general felt like they had to tough things out, especially when it came to mental health. I had enough friends and family members with anxiety to understand a bit about it without needing to quiz Sam about his experience.

It was after nine by the time we rolled out of my place, but the café was jam packed with our neighbors. We headed to the counter and ordered coffees and breakfast sandwiches before scanning the room for open seats.

"Amy! Sam! Over here!"

I looked over to see two women frantically waving at us. They were a little older, maybe mid to late sixties, both stylishly dressed in what looked like Lululemon athleisure.

"Do you know who those women are?" I asked Sam as he groaned underneath his breath.

"Yeah. Let me introduce you."

"Well don't you two look cozy this morning," one of the women said. She was African American with short, cropped hair.

"Hi Monique," Sam greeted her. "Have you met my new neighbor Amy?"

"No, but we've heard *all* about you from Julie." Monique shook my hand in a surprisingly firm grip. "This is my friend Catherine. We both live in your building, one floor down."

"Nice to meet you both," I said politely, surprised I hadn't run into them yet. I'd heard from Julie that these two women seemed to run this place, and they knew everything about everyone.

"Please join us," Monique said, kicking one of the chairs out with her foot.

I glanced at Sam, and he just shrugged in acquiescence. We settled into the other two chairs at the table, and I had the sensation that I'd just joined an inquisition. I wasn't wrong.

"We haven't seen you at yoga class, Amy." Catherine's look seemed to imply that I'd done something wrong. "Maybe you want to come to our Zumba class instead, if that's more your style? Unless you're too busy with Sam to do anything else?"

I glanced over at Sam again, but the coward was staring at the table like he was trying to make himself invisible.

"Sam and I are just friends."

My lie sounded so unconvincing that even I didn't believe me.

"That's not what Mrs. Rothchild says." Catherine and Monique started laughing.

"Who's Mrs. Rothchild?" I asked.

"The woman who interrupted your make out session on the elevator, dear," Catherine said with a disapproving look. "Really, you've been here for weeks now, you should make an effort to meet your neighbors. That's no way to make a first impression."

"Oh, um, sorry, you know I actually work full-time so I've been kind of busy."

Catherine looked at Sam and raised her eyebrows. "Yes, I'm sure you have been."

The two women cackled. Sam pushed up from his chair like someone had just electrified it.

"You know I think I forgot to tell them that we're taking this order to go."

Then the coward practically ran off, leaving me to fend for myself with Monique and Catherine.

"Good job grabbing one of the silver foxes as soon as you moved in," Catherine complimented. I was pretty sure she was staring at Sam's ass as he hurried away.

"It's not like that," I protested.

"You look pretty cozy coming in here," Monique observed.

"I told you, we're just friends," I repeated.

"With benefits I guess," Catherine joked.

I looked around and saw Sam waving at me from the counter, two cups of coffee in his hand. Chickenshit.

"Well, it's nice to finally meet you both," I said politely, inching away from the table. "I should get to our food before it gets cold."

"Hope to see you in class soon," Catherine responded.

"Okay, sure, maybe."

I hustled out the door to where Sam was waiting for me.

"I'm going to get you back for that, you know," I told Sam when we were walking back to our apartments, each of us holding a cardboard cup of coffee. Sam held my hand in one of his hands, our breakfast in the other.

"There's something you need to know about me, Amy," he said solemnly.

"What's that?" I asked.

"I'll always tell you the truth."

"Oh, okay, good." I wasn't sure where he was going with this.

"And the truth is, those two old ladies scare me."

"So you left me alone with them?" I asked, laughing. "What happened to no man left behind?"

He gave my hand a squeeze. "The rules of war don't apply here. But don't worry, I'll make it up to you later."

"Really? How?" I asked skeptically.

"With orgasms. Lots of orgasms."

Sam

Four weeks later...

"Would you come to family dinner with me this Friday?"

Amy lifted her head off my chest, eyes sleepy and hair sticking up in all directions. "What? Why?"

"I'd like to introduce my girlfriend to my family."

She stiffened. "I'm your girlfriend now?"

I couldn't tell how she felt about that. I slid away so I could see her face. We'd been sleeping together for four weeks now, but she was still a bit guarded. She relaxed a little more with me every day though. Amy didn't give her trust easily, and I was relishing the challenge of earning it.

"Aren't you my girlfriend?" I asked, giving her a hard stare.

"I guess I haven't thought about it," she said, a touch of uncertainty in her voice.

"You're my girlfriend," I said firmly. "And my family is dying to meet you. I've never brought anyone to family dinner before you know."

Both my daughter and ex-wife had been bugging me nonstop to invite Amy. They were dying to meet the woman who I couldn't stop talking about.

"No pressure there," she joked weakly. "What exactly happens at these family dinners?"

"Well, we all get together once a month. My daughter and her wife cook a great dinner, and the rest of us eat." I paused. "We talk, play board games, maybe watch a movie. Although sometimes they all gang up on me and tease me about something, unless my son's on leave from the military, then they gang up on him instead."

"Hmm. I don't know about this." I sensed rather than saw her frown.

"Don't worry, they'll love you," I reassured her, taking a stab at figuring out why she seemed hesitant about this.

Amy pushed herself up to seated, shifting so she could face me. I leaned against the headboard across from her, carefully keeping my eyes above her shoulders.

"I'm not worried about people liking me," she finally said. "People's families usually love me. But we've only been...doing whatever this is, for four weeks."

"So?"

"I appreciate the invitation, Sam, truly I do, but we're not nearly at a point where we should be meeting each other's families. It feels like this is all moving a little fast."

Damn it.

"What do you mean?" I asked carefully. "We've been spending a lot of time together over the last month. What feels fast about it?"

"Can't we just continue having fun? Why do we have to get serious and put labels on it and meet families?"

"Because I'm in love with you."

I resisted the urge to slap my hand over my own mouth at that admission. She'd just said we were moving too fast, this was no way to counter that argument. I was such an idiot.

She winced, and I felt a dull pain in my chest.

"Sam. We're not kids anymore. You're a grandfather for god's sake, not a teenager who believes in love at first sight."

I studied her face carefully. Somehow her expression didn't match her words. She didn't look annoyed or even freaked out. She looked scared.

"It's all good," I said, going for casual. "I hear you saying that you're not there yet and I respect that. And if you're not ready to meet my family, that's fine too. You can meet them whenever you're ready. I just want to spend time with you Amy and see where this goes."

She looked slightly suspicious. "So we're good just the way we are for now?"

"Yeah, sure."

It was a gut punch, but I could be patient. Well, maybe I couldn't, because later that day I broached the topic again over dinner.

"Tell me about your previous relationships. We've never talked about this."

Amy stopped with a forkful of meatloaf halfway to her mouth. "What?"

I raised one eyebrow and deepened my voice. "Tell me."

"It's cute the way you think that bossy thing works on me," she said, taking a bite of meatloaf and chewing it carefully. "Why are you asking about this all the sudden?"

"I'm just wondering what in your past is making you nervous about coming to meet my family."

"Not everything has to be about some huge existential wound," she said in a defensive tone. "No one hurt me. I just don't think we've been dating long enough to meet people's family and friends."

"I met Dante and Julie," I reminded her.

"That's different. You already knew them, and they were doing a lame attempt at matchmaking, not sizing you up as a new family member or something."

"Amy. I'd really like to talk about our past relationships. It's something couples do, you know."

She sighed deeply. "How about you start then?" she challenged.

"Fine. My first serious relationship was my senior year of college," I said. "We dated all year and the summer after graduation, but we lived in different cities and soon realized that a long-distance thing wasn't going to work for us. After that I dated a series of women, some for a few months, some for a year or more. No one really seemed like a soulmate or anything. And through it all, there was my best friend, Jane."

I paused to take a bite of my own meal, then continued.

"Jane and I had always joked around that if we were both single when we turned thirty, we'd get married. Then we turned thirty and thought, why not? Neither of us had any good prospects. We were best friends, and that seemed like more of a foundation for a marriage than most couples had. I mean, how many couples do you know that when the passion faded, there was nothing there? We figured we were being smart by having a relationship without all the romantic drama."

"Oh my God," she laughed, "it's like you're describing a scene out of a rom-com."

"Yeah, except there was no friends to lovers situation, just a friends to co-parents thing. We loved each other – we still do – but we were never in love. We never felt romantically attached to each other or anything other than platonic love."

"But you slept together I assume."

"Yes," I acknowledged. "We agreed to be monogamous and while it was never Earth shattering or anything, we were mostly sexually compatible."

Amy winced, and I wondered if it was because it bothered her to think about me with another woman. I would certainly feel the same if the shoe was on the other foot.

"We both wanted to be parents, so we had our son and daughter," I continued. "We were raising them together, and we were both perfectly content with our lives, until Jane met Mark and fell in love with him."

She clasped her hand over her mouth. "Oh my God, your wife was your best friend and she cheated on you?"

"No!" I said quickly. "She told me she was attracted to him when she first met him. We were best friends and we'd always shared everything. So she met Mark and the more time they spent together, the stronger it felt even though they both tried to fight their attraction."

I took another bite of my food, choosing my words carefully.

"When it became clear that their feelings were more than a passing attraction, Jane and I talked about options, including opening up our marriage."

"What, like sharing her?" she interrupted.

"We talked about a few different options, including both of us staying married but dating other people, but in the end we decided to get a divorce," I explained. "Jane and Mark didn't so much as kiss until she was free. He's a good guy, and he absolutely refused to break up her marriage or do anything that would be considered cheating until Jane and I had filed for divorced."

"So you two broke up a perfectly good marriage just in case this other guy who she hadn't even kissed was a better match for her?"

Amy sounded incredulous. She wasn't the first person to have this reaction.

"No, we broke up a perfectly good marriage so one of us could be with their true love."

"True love? That sounds like something from a fairy tale."

"It's not," I said, staring at her. "But if it was, I'd tell you that Jane and Mark are living happily ever after now. They're perfect for each other, and Mark's become like a brother to me. My kids love him too."

She shook her head. "Wow, modern relationships," she mumbled.

I got it. Jane and I had a weird story. It was exceedingly unusual for a husband to willingly divorce his wife so she could see if another guy was her soul mate. It was even rarer that two people could be good friends before the wedding, during the marriage, and after the divorce. But Jane and I hadn't missed a beat in our friendship, and I was extremely grateful for that.

"Now what about you?" I asked. "Tell me about your dating history."

"I was a serial monogamist most of my life," she said. "Then when I turned forty I said to myself, Amy why are you doing this? You're too old to have kids, you don't even want to be married, why not have fun? You should date more and just enjoy your single life."

"And are you?" I asked, making a vow to myself that I'd change her mind about being married. This woman was going to be wearing my ring if it was the last thing I did.

"Am I what?"

"Having fun? Enjoying your single life?"

"I thought I was. But dating is exhausting, you know? And I have to admit that sometimes I've found myself dating a guy mostly because I'm bored or lonely, not because I particularly liked him. I know it sounds terrible, but it is what it is."

We ate in silence for a few minutes before Amy spoke again. "Okay, I'll go."

"Go where?"

"To your family dinner. But don't make a big thing about it," she warned.

"I wouldn't dream of it."

Amy

"How's everything going with Sam?"

The next day was unseasonably warm, and Julie had convinced me to go down to Silver Falls' outdoor pool. It was heated both inside the pool and around the perimeter, but I couldn't stand the thought of going when it was below freezing. A day in the fifties seemed a little more doable.

"It's going okay," I said, careful to keep my voice neutral.

"What?" Julie asked.

"What what?" I countered.

"Please, I know you, Ames. What's wrong? Are you bored with him already or something?"

"God no."

"Is the sex bad?" she guessed.

"The sex is good," I confirmed. "Very very good."

"Yeah I heard that from Monique and Catherine," Julie laughed. "At length."

I stopped dead. "What?"

"They said that your downstairs neighbors claim they can hear you having loud sex at all hours."

"I doubt that," I said, making a mental note to tell Sam we needed to quiet down. We could get kind of loud, but I didn't realize anyone else could hear us. Besides, we usually fell into an exhausted sleep by one a.m. at the latest. After all, I had to work most mornings.

"So what's the problem?" Julie asked.

"He wants me to meet his family."

"Wow, big step."

"He says he's in love with me," I shared.

Julie came to a dead stop. "He told you he loves you?"

"Yeah." I started walking again and she followed my lead.

"That's perfect." Julie was practically gushing.

"Why is that perfect?" I asked crankily.

"Because you're in love with him too." She said this like it was obvious and I was an idiot if I didn't know it was obvious.

"I don't know how I feel," I hedged.

"Sure you do. I've been your best friend for over forty years, I know when you're in love."

"I've never been in love before," I reminded her.

"Yeah, that's how I can tell this time is different."

***

"Amy! It's so nice to finally meet you!"

The young woman who opened the door pulled me into a hug. I lifted my arm just in time, narrowly avoiding spilling apple cobbler on her.

"I'm Penny, Sam's daughter."

She had dark hair and dark eyes just like her father. As we pulled away from each other, we subtly sized each other up. When Penny gave me another smile, I had a feeling that I'd passed the first test.

"Grandpa!"

We were interrupted by three little kids racing into the room and throwing themselves at Sam. He dropped to his knees and pulled them all into a hug.

"Hi girls. This is my friend Miss Amy."

Sam pointed at the oldest girl, who looked to be about eight years old. "This is Amelia. And this is Marielle," he said, pointing at a smaller version of the first girl, this one looked to be about six. "And this," he picked up a little girl who was darker and much smaller than the other two, "is my little peanut, Rebecca."

"Nice to meet you all," I said.

The younger two girls kept their attention on their grandfather, but the older one gave me a shrewd look. "Are you my grandpa's girlfriend?" she asked.

I couldn't tell how she felt about that.

Penny patted her head. "Amelia, it's rude to be nosy."

"It's okay. Yes, I guess I am your grandpa's girlfriend."

It was the first time I'd set it out loud, to Sam or anyone, and he sent me a wide smile that promised to reward me later. I shivered.

"Well, come on in and meet the rest of the family," Penny said.

We followed her into the house, meeting Sam's ex-wife Jane and her husband Mark, as well as Penny's wife, Monica. Monica and Jane were busy in the kitchen making dinner, refusing any assistance from the rest of us, so Sam and I settled in the living room with his daughter and Mark. Penny brought us each a drink, and the girls disappeared to play before dinner.

Penny and Monica had a lovely home, clean but slightly chaotic in the way that a house with several younger kids would be. I remembered those days from when Julie's kids were little.

I'd wanted kids when I was younger but when I didn't meet the right guy, I gradually accepted that it wasn't going to happen for me. I could have adopted or tried artificial insemination, but I decided that being the slightly crazy aunt to Julie's kids was good enough. I'd never regretted the decision not to be a single mother, not after I saw how much of a struggle it was for Julie.

Looking around at the toys scattered around the room, I realized that if I'd had kids I'd likely be a grandmother now, or close to it. It was a sobering thought for a woman who still thought of herself as being in her twenties.

As if he instinctively knew I needed comfort, Sam draped his arm around my shoulder and pulled me closer to him on the couch. Penny sent us an indulgent smile.

"You guys are so cute together."

"So, how did you two meet?" Monica asked us a little while later. "I don't think I heard the story."

We were all crowded around a long table, so close that Sam's leg pressed against mine. He settled his hand on my thigh and gave me a little squeeze. We exchanged a glance.

"There's no story really," I said. "I recently moved in next door. Sam and I kept running into each other, and my best friend was trying to fix us up as well, so we started dating."

"You're getting a good guy here," Jane spoke up. "Sam is kind, clean, reliable and pretty low maintenance."

Penny laughed. "Mom, you're making him sound like a used car."

"All I'm saying is that it's pretty rare to get a recommendation from a guy's ex-wife."

"I'll keep that in mind," I assured Jane.

The rest of the night passed quickly. Sam's family was great, welcoming and inclusive without being too pushy or overly nosy. They put me at ease right away.

After a delicious dinner we stayed for an after-dinner drink, then headed back to Silver Falls, both of us quiet as we made the drive home. One of the things I liked about Sam was that he wasn't one of those people who seemed compelled to fill in every silence with chatter. Our silences were comfortable and companionable, and when one of us spoke, it was because we actually had something to say.

"Do you want to sleep over?" Sam asked as we entered the elevator to our building.

"Hold the door!" we heard someone call before I could answer.

Sam pressed the button, and Mrs. Rothchild shuffled in, her scary looking little dog trailing on a leash.

"Good evening," Sam greeted her, turning on the charm and giving her his warmest smile.

Behind the old woman's back I rolled my eyes. Her head snapped around as if she could tell what I was doing, and I gave her a smile of my own.

"Nice night, huh?" I strove for casual.

"Yes," she snipped, staring at the door like she could will the elevator to go faster using just her mind.

We stopped at her floor, and as soon as the doors closed behind her, we both burst out laughing.

"She's never going to get over catching us making out," I said.

"No, I guess not," Sam agreed.

"Good thing she won't know about this," I said.

I pressed the stop button and Sam's eyes widened as the elevator lurched to a stop between floors.

"What are you doing, Amy?" His voice was suddenly hoarse.

"You've been half hard since dinner," I said, moving closer and dropping to my knees in front of him. "I've wanted to do this all night."

Sam made a gurgling noise like maybe he'd swallowed his tongue. Feminine power surged in my veins.

I reached for his belt, making quick work of unbuckling him before unzipping his khakis. I pulled his pants open and slid his boxers down just enough to release his cock and balls. Wrapping my fingers around him, I gave him a few rough pumps, getting him ready for me.

It didn't take much, probably because we'd spent the entire night pressed against each other, our bodies always touching in some way, keeping us both in a state of low level arousal.

I leaned forward and kissed the very tip of his dick before slowly moving my head forward and taking him fully into my mouth. I pulled back just as slowly, lightly grazing him with my teeth, before pushing forward again.

Sam gripped the railing on the side of the elevator with one hand and my hair in the other. I ceded control as he started thrusting into my mouth at his own pace, pushing forward until he tapped the back of my throat, then pulling back. I could feel him growing thicker and harder in my mouth, so I knew he was close to his release. I reached down and cupped his balls in my hand, giving them a gentle squeeze.

Sam groaned loudly, his hips snapping forward and back faster now. When I moved my other hand around his hip and slipped one finger between his ass cheeks he stiffened, then jerked forward roughly. He groaned again as he released several spurts of cum down my throat. I swallowed furiously, wanting to catch every salty drop.

When he stepped back, Sam looked a little dazed.

"Wow."

"Yeah," I said, wiping my mouth with my hand and then rising to my feet. "Are we going to your place then?"

"Fuck yeah."

Sam

I was finishing up a session with a client when I heard a knock on the door.

I glanced at my watch, seeing that it was almost time for Amy to come over. It was Valentine's Day and I'd convinced her that we should celebrate our new relationship status by going out for a romantic dinner.

"Do you want me to let them in, Sam?" my client asked.

"Yes please," I said, figuring that Amy had come over early. "I'm just going to email this spreadsheet to you so you can review it before we meet next week."

"Thanks Sam."

I heard the murmur of voices in the hall, then I looked up to see Amy walking in the door. I tilted my head in confusion when I saw she was wearing a long puffy coat that zipped from her knees to her neck. Her legs were bare, and she was wearing flip flops.

"What are you—?"

My words stuttered off as Amy unzipped her jacket and shrugged it off her shoulders, revealing her deliciously curvy body beneath. She was wearing a red lace teddy that cut high on the hips and low in the front, showing off lots of pale white skin.

"Holy. Shit."

"Do you like my new outfit?" she teased, making her voice low and sultry. "I got it as a Valentine's Day present for you."

"Oh, I more than like it," I said approvingly. "It's the best Valentine's Day present I ever received."

I appreciated the gesture, but I also recognized it as more than Amy showing off her new lingerie. I knew her well enough now to know that this was a statement. She was all in. Things were moving to the next level with us. My heart swelled with happiness.

Amy walked closer to the desk and quirked one eyebrow.

"Have I ever told you about my fantasy?" she asked.

I shook my head. All the blood in my body had headed south of my belt when she shrugged off that jacket, and my brain synapses were no longer firing properly.

She took another step, setting her palms on the desk and bending at the waist. Her breasts strained against the delicate fabric, and I couldn't help but stare.

"Ever since the first time I saw this office, I had a fantasy about you laying me over the desk like this...," she lowered her belly onto the desk, propping her head up on her hands. "Then you lean over me and take me from behind, nice and rough."

My chair squeaked loudly as I pushed it away from the desk and practically leapt to my feet. As I raced around to the other side, I thanked every god in the heavens for bringing me this woman, especially when I realized that the back of the teddy was just a thong.

Coming behind her, I stroked the soft skin of Amy's bare ass. It was so pale and perfect I couldn't help but bring my palm down and give her a little smack. She jolted in surprise.

"Oh!"

"Is that okay?" I asked, my dick already so hard it was practically bursting out from behind my zipper.

"Yeah," she breathed. "Do it again."

I did, and she made a little moaning noise that I took for encouragement.

"You've been a bad girl," I said in my deepest voice.

Amy smirked at me over her shoulder.

"Maybe you should spank me some more," she said in a soft, breathy voice. "Just to make sure I learned my lesson."

I smacked her ass a few more times, the skin flushing pink as I covered the surface with quick spanks. I'd never hit a woman in my life, never even thought about spanking someone, but damned if I hadn't just unlocked a kink I didn't even know I had.

I slid my fingers between Amy's legs and found her dripping wet. Clearly I wasn't the only one who was enjoying this little game.

"You like this," I said, sliding my finger through her folds and spreading her moisture.

"Yeah. And so do you."

I grabbed my cock with one hand, her hip with my other. "Are you ready?"

"God, yeah," she sighed.

I shifted the fabric of her thong to one side, then pushed into her with one long thrust. Both of us sighed when my hips met her ass. Gripping Amy's round hips, I began pounding in and out of her, setting a steady pace, experiencing a primal urge to mark her inside the same way I'd marked her on the outside with my hand. Every thrust lifted her up on her tiptoes, and I enjoyed having total control.

"Sam! I'm close," Amy gasped.

I lowered my body over hers, trapping her between me and the desk, increasing the strength of my thrusts until I felt Amy's inner muscles tighten around me. The instant her orgasm overtook her I shifted back upright. She spasmed beneath me almost violently, but I was too far gone to pay attention. I couldn't hold back as my own orgasm raced through my body. I pushed in as deep as I could and released my cum inside her womb.

When I was finished, I sagged back down, covering her body with mine, running kisses along her shoulders as we both recovered.

"That was a hell of a Valentine's Day present. You should come to my office more often," I said, nipping at her ear lobe.

"Next time we should play teacher and student," she said.

My cock twitched inside her channel even though it had already gone soft.

"I guess you like that idea," she teased.

"Maybe we should think about a second round," I said, pulling out of her and helping her to her feet.

I'd completely forgotten that we had dinner reservations. If Amy remembered, she didn't say anything.

"Really? So quickly?" Amy pretended to be impressed. "I had no idea an old man like you could still go that much."

"I'll show you how much I can go," I joked, grabbing her by the waist and throwing her over my shoulder.

She squealed against my back. "Put me down before you hurt yourself," she laughed.

I punched in the code on the door that separated my office area from the rest of the apartment, strode into the living room, and tossed her on the couch. Amy wiggled out of her teddy, tossing it over her head.

After ripping off the rest of my clothes, I levered down on top of her, covering her with my body. I crashed my mouth into hers, giving Amy a hard, claiming kiss.

It had been years since I'd felt this much desperate lust around anyone, and even then, it had never been as strong as what I had with Amy. I couldn't get enough of her. After a multi-year dry spell, she had single handedly kicked my libido back into gear.

I slid between her legs, lined up our bodies, and slid inside her heat. We both groaned in pleasure as I started to move in and out.

"Harder Sam, harder!"

I increased the pace of my thrusts as Amy wrapped her legs around mine and lifted her hips to meet me, perfectly in sync. It didn't take long until she was shuddering beneath me, thank God, because I couldn't last much longer.

"I'm coming."

My voice sounded low and gravelly as I gave in to my second orgasm in less than fifteen minutes, possibly a new record.

"Amy!"

I arched my back, sliding my hips in a scooping motion so I could rub against her clit while I came, hoping to get Amy to a third orgasm along the way.

Suddenly my entire body jolted, and an intense pain burned through my back and down to my hip. What the hell? It felt like someone had just stabbed me in the back.

"Ah!"

My arms gave out and I fell on top of Amy, then rolled right off onto the floor, fortunately just missing the coffee table. Red hot pain made it hard to breathe and I curled into a fetal position. Amy stared down at me in shocked horror.

"Sam, what is it? Is it your heart?"

I squeezed my eyes shut, trying to block out the pain.

"No."

"What's wrong then?" she asked.

"I don't know, but I think you broke me."

Amy

"What happened?"

The extremely young paramedic looked from Sam, who was still moaning in a fetal position on the floor, to me. I'd thrown a blanket over Sam, and I was wearing my puffy coat again, sweating bullets in the warm room. Out of the corner of my eye I could see my red teddy still draped over the back of the couch.

"We were, um, well we were having sex and all the sudden he fell over in pain."

He whipped around towards Sam, exchanging a look with the other paramedic.

"Sir, do you feel any pressure in your chest? Any tightness or pain?"

My face burned but I couldn't say if it was from embarrassment or because I was wearing this damned jacket. I sidled over to the couch and grabbed the teddy, stuffing it into my coat pocket.

"No, the pain is all in my back. It feels like someone stabbed me."

The other paramedic took Sam's blood pressure and pulse. My poor boyfriend looked terrible. His face was ashen with pain, his eyes screwed shut as he curled into a ball like a sleepy puppy.

"BP's a little high, but nothing serious," the paramedic on the floor reported to his partner.

"Is he on any blood pressure medicine?" Doogie Paramedic asked me.

"I have no idea."

Damn. Wasn't this something I should know as his girlfriend? I remembered seeing him take pills before, but I had no idea what they were for. We'd only been dating for a short time, we'd never talked about our health histories before.

"Sam!" I called. "They need to know if you're on any medications?"

"Yeah, all of my meds are in the kitchen cabinet, next to the refrigerator."

I ran into the kitchen, returning with three prescription bottles that the young paramedic dutifully typed into his tablet.

"What's wrong with him?" I asked the paramedics when they seemed to be finished with their exam.

"Could be a lot of things, we'll have to have the doctors check him out," Doogie hedged. "We're going to take him into the ER at Denver Health, they're the only ones who are taking admissions right now."

"I'll go with you."

Doogie held up one hand. "Sorry ma'am, unless you're his wife we can't take you with us on the bus."

I was filled with a sudden fury. "But I can't leave him alone!"

"You're going to have to, ma'am. Rules are rules." He turned to his coworker. "Let's get him on the gurney and hit the road."

I was only able to stand by helplessly while they slid a back board under Sam and lifted him onto the gurney. He groaned in pain with every single jostle.

"Sam, honey, I'll meet you at the hospital, okay?"

I leaned down and pressed a quick kiss on his cheek, afraid to touch him anywhere else.

"Okay," he whispered softly.

As soon as they rolled Sam out of his apartment I burst into tears. He'd been fine before he collapsed, so I had no idea what could be wrong with him. I was worried sick.

Shaking with a combination of fear and adrenaline, I was doubtful about my ability to drive. Grabbing my phone, I headed next door to put on some clothes. I called Julie on my way out.

"Hey, it's me," I sobbed. "I know it's Valentine's Day and you and Dante were probably going to do something romantic, but I really need a favor."

Ninety minutes later I sat in the waiting room with Julie and Dante, feeling nauseous with worry. The people at the desk had stubbornly refused to tell us anything about Sam's condition. Due to privacy rules, the hospital couldn't even confirm that Sam was there, though we knew the ambulance had brought him.

I couldn't even call Sam to get an update since he'd been buck naked when they wheeled him away and didn't have his phone.

We looked up as Jane and Mark came racing into the waiting area, skidding to a stop when she saw us.

"Oh, Amy, you are here. The hospital called me because I'm listed as Sam's next of kin. How is he?"

"I don't know, they won't tell me anything." My eyes filled up with tears again.

She grabbed my hand, pulling me to my feet. "Come with me, we'll find out what's going on."

After Jane showed her ID card, the clerk acknowledged that Sam was on site and promised to have someone come out and update us. We waited another fifteen minutes before a woman in scrubs came out and called Jane's name.

"Hi, I'm Doctor Freidman."

"How is he?" Jane and I asked at the same time.

The woman looked between us curiously but didn't ask any questions.

"He's resting now. I can let one person back to see him. It's up to him how much he wants to share about his condition."

"You go, Amy," Jane said. "I'll wait with your friends. Just let us know what you find out."

I sent her a grateful look. "Thank you, Jane, I really appreciate it."

I followed the doctor back to a cubicle. Sam was propped up on a gurney, an IV in his arm and an oxygen tube coming out of his nose. When he saw me, he gave me a huge smile.

"Oh, there's my love! My girlfriend! Amy! Hi love! Hi Amy!"

I rushed to his side and grabbed his hand. He looked a little manic, his eyes wide and pupils dilated.

"Sam, how are you feeling, honey?"

"They gave me medicine, all the medicine," he said loudly. "It's so nice! I feel like I'm floating. I love medicine. I love you, Amy!"

I looked at the doctor in alarm and she gave me a whisper of a smile.

"He's had a pretty high dose of muscle relaxants as well as pain meds. He's probably going to be loopy for a while."

She looked at Sam.

"Mr. Amatto, is it okay for me to talk to this lady about what's wrong with you?"

"She's not a lady, Amy's my love. I'm going to ask her to marry me someday, but don't tell her, okay? It's a surprise."

I rolled my lips in to keep from laughing. Sam was hilarious when he was high on meds.

"I'm assuming you were with him when the, uh, accident happened?"

I nodded. "Yes."

"The good news is that Mr. Amatto doesn't have a major injury. It's basically a severe muscle pull in the back that exacerbated an old disc injury and caused a significant amount of nerve pain. He needs to take it easy for a few days, do some gentle stretching, and use things like ice and Epsom salts to help keep the inflammation down. If someone will be with him tonight I'll go ahead and discharge him."

"Yes, I will be with him," I reassured her.

"Great. One suggestion, he might want to warm up the muscles before sex. Anything too strenuous or acrobatic might aggravate the injury again."

My face flamed, even though I had nothing to be embarrassed about. Surely people got injured during sex all the time, right? At least we hadn't been playing with some toy that got stuck, that would have been even worse.

"We'll be more careful in the future," I reassured her.

"I'll send a nurse in to take out his IV and give you his discharge instructions, then you can take him home."

"Thank you, Doctor."

"Amy! Amy!" Sam called from his bed as the doctor exited.

I turned and stroked his hair away from his forehead, feeling a combination of relief that Sam was okay and surprise at how worried I'd been about him. My feelings for him ran deeper than I even knew. Being banned from seeing him or even getting any information while he'd been back here alone and in pain had been even more upsetting than the injury itself. At least for me. I'd never felt so helpless.

"You're my love," Sam said dreamily.

"I know, and you're mine. Remind me to tell you that again some time when you're not high as a kite."

Sam

I spent the next three days on the couch in my living room being pampered by Amy. It was kind of nice. Other than the back pain part of course. The anti-inflammatories did their job and along with gentle stretching I was able to feel almost normal by day four. Normal enough to think about making breakfast...

"What are you doing?"

I glanced over my shoulder at Amy. Since the couch felt more comfortable on my back, she'd been sleeping in my bed the last few nights so she could be close by if I needed her. She'd even brought her laptop over here and worked from my dining room table so she could keep an eye on me.

"I'm scrambling some eggs."

She rushed over. "Let me do it."

I checked her with my hip, relieved when the movement felt pain free.

"No way. I'm about ninety percent better and you've been taking care of me for several days now. Pour yourself a cup of coffee and sit your cute little ass down while I cook us breakfast."

Mumbling under her breath, Amy followed my instructions. She sat in a chair and watched my every move, no doubt ready to pounce if I needed her.

A few minutes later I brought over two plates piled high with scrambled eggs and sausage links. It wasn't the most heart healthy meal, but then again I needed protein to recover from my back injury. At least that's what I told myself.

"How's your pain?" Amy asked solicitously.

"Almost non-existent," I replied honestly. "I did my stretching routine this morning and I didn't even need any pain killers after. In another day or two I'll be as good as new."

"You do look like you're walking easier," Amy acknowledged.

"I can tell the difference for sure," I agreed, handing her a plate. "Now eat up."

She rolled her eyes at my bossy tone but picked up her fork. We ate in silence for a few minutes.

"Thanks for taking care of me, Amy," I said a few minutes later. "It means a lot."

"It's no problem, after all, I was at least partly responsible."

"Partly responsible?" I teased. "I think it's at least seventy-five percent your fault."

"How is it my fault?" she protested. "I was on the bottom. You're the one who tried to do the fancy moves."

"Yeah, but you started everything by coming over wearing just your puffy coat and that tiny red teddy," he reminded me. "I was too distracted by your naked body to think clearly."

"Oh yeah."

Her cheeks pinked up at the memory. It was adorable.

"What happened to that teddy anyway?" I asked. "I want to see it again after I'm fully recovered."

"I think it's still in my coat pocket."

"Talking about that teddy reminds me that we need to remember to erase the video."

Amy frowned. "What video?"

"I have a motion activated recording system in that office. Everything that happens in there gets recorded."

Amy's fork dropped to the table with a clatter. "What? Why?"

"Since I work with vulnerable women in a private space, my attorney recommended having all clients sign a recording waiver as a condition of service," I explained. "That way if there are any allegations, we have proof of what really happened."

Amy looked horrified.

"Please tell me no one else has access to those recordings."

I debated teasing her but decided to tell her the truth.

"It records directly into my cloud storage. Only I can see it. Although maybe we should save it..."

"Sam! Promise me you will delete that tape right away!"

I couldn't help but laugh at her stern expression. "Tape? You're aging yourself, sweetheart."

She glared at me until I relented. "I promise we'll delete it right after breakfast. Unless you want to watch it first?"

Amy paused, the wheels in her brain turning.

"When are you cleared for sex again?" she asked.

"One more week if I continue to heal okay."

"Let's hold onto it then," she decided. "We can watch it together before you erase it."

I raised one eyebrow. "You're a dirty girl, aren't you?"

"You know it."

"By the way, I'm no longer high as a kite," I told her, leaning forward on my elbows to meet her gaze.

"Yeah, so?" She looked confused.

"You were planning to tell me you loved me when I wasn't as high as a kite."

"You remember that?" she asked in surprise.

"Of course."

"You didn't remember what year it was when the nurse tested you for cognition before they discharged you."

"You're more important than a calendar," I said solemnly. "Come on now, tell me you love me now that I'm sober enough to enjoy it."

She sighed in exasperation.

"Fine. I love you Sam, okay?"

My heart soared, literally soared, hearing her say it out loud. Given how strongly the medications had hit me, I hadn't been one hundred percent certain she'd really said she loved me at the hospital until now.

"It's more than okay. I love you too. Now, how about you come sit on my lap?"

"No way. I've already been embarrassed once with those baby paramedics. I'm not taking a chance on your delicate body getting injured again so soon."

"A kiss then?" I bargained.

"Fine, I'll give you a kiss. But no funny business until you're totally healed."

She got up and walked around the table, looping her arms around my shoulders and leaning in towards me. Her expression was tender.

"I love you Sam, and I'm glad you didn't have a heart attack or break your penis during sex like I was afraid we did."

"You say the sweetest things," I teased, bringing my lips closer to hers.

"Do you want sweet, or do you want real?" she asked.

"I want *you*," I said firmly, staring into her eyes.

"You've got me. Forever."

It was one of the happiest moments of my life. But then I had to go and open my big mouth and mess things up again.

"As long as you're feeling generous, how would you feel about moving in with me?"

She smacked me lightly on the side of my head with her palm.

"Are you sure you didn't injure your brain when you fell? What's wrong with you? I'm not moving in with you after dating for like six weeks."

"You can't blame a guy for trying," I said.

"Yeah, well, try again after we've got more time on the books."

"Oh I will, love. I will."

Epilogue – Amy

One year later, Valentine's Day

"Are you and Sam getting married on Valentine's Day so he'll remember your anniversary date?" Jane asked.

I shook my head. "No, it's so I will."

My soon-to-be husband was much more romantic and sentimental than I was.

Jane shook her head.

"You two really are a perfect match." Her face turned serious. "I just want to say how happy I am for you, for both of you. Sam's a great guy, my best friend since we were kids, and I'm thrilled that he's finally found the kind of love I have with Mark. Welcome to our family."

"Thanks Jane, that means a lot to me."

Penny stuck her head into the room where I was getting ready for the wedding ceremony.

"Mom! You're the woman of honor, you should be helping the groom!"

Jane rolled her eyes. "The groom has it easy. All he has to do is put on a suit and comb his hair. Amy has more work to do."

"Hey!" I protested with a laugh. "What are you saying?"

"You know what I mean, you're gorgeous of course, but you still have to do your make-up and hair."

"Is it time to do the make-up?" Julie breezed in, her daughter Abby right behind her.

Julie's kids were like my own, so I'd made sure to make them part of the wedding ceremony. Jane was standing up for Sam and Julie was my maid of honor, and we had Penny, Sam's son Paul, Abby, and Julie's son Scott responsible for different parts of the event so that everyone was involved.

We'd opted to do a small wedding at the Silver Falls Community Center with just our families and closest friends, but after the wedding dinner we were opening up the room for any community members who wanted to join us for dessert and coffee courtesy of Dante.

Last summer, after six months of dating, Sam finally convinced me to move in with him. It was a little cozy, especially on the days we both worked at home, but we were making it work.

My moving out freed up Julie's apartment which she'd rented to Muriel, a mutual friend of ours who had just gotten divorced after twenty years of marriage. The timing worked out perfectly for everyone.

Julie, Muriel, and I had a standing coffee and walking date every week to help us keep up with each other. Sometimes Catherine and Monique joined us, updating us on all the gossip and activities in our tight knit community. I'd grown to love Silver Fox Falls during my time living here.

The first time Sam asked me to marry him I said no, but I'd agreed to move in with him as a compromise. The second time he asked I said no again and told him we should talk about it in the future. The third time he stuck a ring on my finger while I was still half asleep and ordered me to marry him.

The third time was the charm.

After the wedding we were planning to go to one of those all-inclusive resorts in Mexico and just soak up the warm weather after a long Denver winter. I'd already told Sam that he needed to be extra careful when we had honeymoon sex, because there was no way I was going to explain to Mexican doctors that my new husband had a tendency to throw out his back if he moved the wrong way.

Abby and Julie finished my makeup, then Penny headed into the main room to let them know we were ready to get started with the ceremony.

"Are you ready?" Julie asked as we heard the music start in the next room.

"Yeah, I am."

I was surprisingly calm for a woman who was about to get married for the first time at fifty-seven.

Julie gave me a quick hug. "Let's go get you hitched."

The wedding march started as Julie and I reached the back of the room. Everyone stood up to watch me walk up the aisle, but I only had eyes for the smiling silver fox waiting for me in the front. Our eyes met and he mouthed, "I love you."

I was the luckiest woman in the world, I thought as I mouthed back, "I love you, too."

***

Hey there! If you liked this book, please show me some love, and leave a review. Good reviews are like puppies, they make everyone feel happy.

If you'd like another fun story about a midlife couple falling in love at the holidays, keep reading for a special excerpt from "Dropping the Ball[1]," an opposites attract workplace romance available everywhere now.

---

1.   https://books2read.com/DroppingBall

Special Preview

Dropping the Ball by Rose Bak

I looked around the crowded conference room and resisted the urge to crawl under the table in embarrassment. I was a highly trained Special Agent with the FBI and somehow I'd managed to not only get myself kidnapped, but also had to be rescued by a damn civilian. An older, plus-size civilian who'd been impersonating me and from the looks of it, sleeping with the guy who was supposed to be my new partner.

What did it say about my life that I was gone for more than two days and none of my colleagues had even noticed that I was gone?

The civilian – also named Michelle—had somehow retrieved a key piece of evidence from a mob boss, knocked him out with a bowling trophy, disarmed one of his thugs, and rescued both myself and Derrick Hayes, a detective with the Seattle Police Department who was supposed to be working the case with me. Although why he thought the civilian was me was beyond comprehension. She got winded running a block!

I gave in and rubbed my temples a few times, hoping it would at least make my headache go away.

The room quieted as my boss, Supervisory Special Agent Gary Fencik, strode into the room with the air of authority that always surrounded him.

Just like every time I saw Gary, my heart sped up the tiniest bit. He was a good ten years older than me, around forty-five, with brown hair cut in one of those nondescript FBI haircuts pretty much everyone here wore. Over the past year, streaks of silver had started to appear mixed between the brown strands. Not that I studied him carefully or anything...

Because it was a holiday weekend he was dressed casually in faded jeans and a navy blue FBI tee shirt that hugged his broad shoulders and the muscled planes of his hard chest.

The second he breached the door his eyes went right to me, concern and regret flashing in their brown depths.

He strode over to my chair, forcing me to look up at him. I had a quick vision of other things I could do that would require me to look up at him from below, then I ruthlessly squashed that thought the same way I did every time I was tempted to think of him as anything other than my supervisor.

That's right, I was a damn cliché. A single career woman hopelessly in love with her boss.

"Are you okay Michelle?" he asked me softly. He'd never called me by my first name before.

"We were worried when we heard they found you out at the warehouse. With the name confusion between you and the civilian over there, we had no idea that you were missing. I'm so sorry."

I was surprised at how emotional he sounded. For just a second, I let myself believe his interest was more than professional. Then a flush climbed my cheeks as I reminded myself that we had an audience. I gave him a nod and kept my voice neutral.

"I'm fine, Gary."

The professional mask slipped back into place, and he turned away from me to start the debriefing.

***

For more of Gary and Michelle's story check out "Dropping the Ball[1]", a midlife workplace romance.

You can read about the other Michelle's adventures falling in love with Derrick in "Faking It With the Detective[2]".

---

1. https://books2read.com/DroppingBall

2.   https://books2read.com/FakingDetective

Both these books are available now at select retailers. For more information on this and other books, visit my website at bit.ly/AuthorRoseBak[3].

---

3.   https://books2read.com/ap/RDOk1w/Rose-Bak

Other Books by Rose Bak

Silver Fox Falls Series
    Unexpected Gift
    Unexpected Love
Boozy Book Club Series
    Beach Reads
    Bubbly & Billionaires
    Martinis & Mysteries
    Bourbon & Bikers
    Midlife Madness
    Extra Innings
    The Proposal Solution
Midlife Crisis Contemporary Romance Series
    Summer Wedding
    Roasting with Rob
    Christmas Punch
    Disaster Planning
    Second Chance to Score
    Factory Reset
    Saving Texas
    Texas Christmas
    Canadian Doctor
    Tempted at Midnight
The Good with Numbers Holiday Romance Series
    Love Unmasked
    The Thanksgiving Scrooge
    Maid for Christmas
    Countdown to Love
    Valentine's Lottery
    Christmas Angel
Loving the Holidays Contemporary Romance Series

Dating Santa
New Year's Steve
Independence Dave
Comfort & Joy
Faking It with the Detective
Dropping the Ball
Island Getaway
The Oliver Boys Band Contemporary Romance Series
Until You Came Along
Rock Star Teacher
Rock Star Writer
Rock Star Neighbor
Rock Star Lawyer
Magical Midlife Series
Beltane Magic (prequel)
Love Potion
Psychic Flashes
Halloween Surprise
Giant Love
Kitchen Magic
Alien Feeling
Bite-Sized Shifters Paranormal Romance Series
Long Distance Wolf
Wolf Doctor
Kat's Dog
Designer Wolf
Wolf Sheriff
Cocktail Wolf
Second Chance Wolf
Runaway Wolf
Holidays with the Shifters Series
Santa's Claws

Bear Humbug
Jingle Bear
Silver Paws
Joy to the Wolf
Lion's Heart
The Diamond Bay Contemporary Romance Series
Brand New Penny
Fresh as a Daisy
Right as Rain
Reunited Series
Together Again
Finding My Baby
King of the Reunion
Caught by My Best Friend
Standalones
Beach Wedding
Jessie's Girl
Non-fiction
What to Do If You Find a Cougar in Your Living Room: Self-Care in an Uncaring World

It's All About Relationships: Reflections on Love, Friendship, and Connection

Catch up with these and other stories coming soon. Join my newsletter for more information[1] or follow my author page on your favorite retailer.

---

1. *https://storyoriginapp.com/giveaways/62ee758e-068f-11eb-904e-c373f6014fe1*

About the Author

Rose Bak has been obsessed with books since she got her first library card at age five. She is a passionate reader with an e-reader bursting with thousands of beloved books.

Although Rose enjoys writing both fiction and nonfiction, romance novels have always been her favorite guilty pleasure, both as a reader and an author. Rose's contemporary romance books focus on strong female characters over thirty-five and the alpha males who love them. Expect a lot of steam, a little bit of snark, and a guaranteed happily ever after.

Rose lives in the Pacific Northwest with her family, and special needs dogs. In addition to writing, she also teaches accessible yoga and loves music. Sadly, she has absolutely no musical talent, so she mostly sings in the shower.

Please sign up for the Rose Bak Romance newsletter[1] to get a free book and keep up to date on all the latest news. You can also follow Rose on Facebook[2], Instagram[3], Twitter[4], Goodreads[5], or Bookbub[6].

---

1. https://storyoriginapp.com/giveaways/62ee758e-068f-11eb-904e-c373f6014fe1

2. https://www.facebook.com/AuthorRoseBak

3. https://www.instagram.com/authorrosebak/

4. https://twitter.com/AuthorRoseBak

5. https://www.goodreads.com/authorrosebak

6. https://www.bookbub.com/authors/rose-bak

Don't miss out!

Visit the website below and you can sign up to receive emails whenever Rose Bak publishes a new book. There's no charge and no obligation.

https://books2read.com/r/B-A-VATM-JHXXC

BOOKS 2 READ

Connecting independent readers to independent writers.

www.ingramcontent.com/pod-product-compliance
Lightning Source LLC
Chambersburg PA
CBHW031434130726
47989CB00003B/1136